Dana Diehl

The Earth Room

a short story collection

Black Lawrence Press

For the glaciers, the forests, the caves,
the sky islands, and the cabins in the woods.

Black Lawrence Press

Executive Editor: Diane Goettel
Book Cover Design: Zoe Norvell
Book Interior Design: Serena Solin
Cover Art: "Circa 1903" by Brooke Sauer

ISBN: 9781625573001

Published 2026 by Black Lawrence Press.

Printed in the United States.

Contents

Always Night

A SHARD OF TOOTH drops from my mouth into my hand. The break feels clean, permanent. I feel around with my tongue, searching for the empty space it left behind. I notice one of my back molars is angular in a way it wasn't before. It has a sharp point, like a carnivore's.

Somewhere below me is the southern edge of Iceland. The plane moves through the night, folding time, collapsing eight hours of darkness into three, and I can't sleep. The man in the seat next to me, a thirty-something with skinny thighs, is slumped and snoring. His shoulder presses against mine. I can imagine biting into his exposed neck with my sharpened molar, drawing blood before he even wakes.

I switch on my reading light and examine the piece of tooth in my hand. Nothing seems wrong with it at all. It's like I've simply shed it, like a strand of hair. I place the shard of tooth in the front pocket of my jeans, and it disappears behind the denim, weightless.

I check my watch. There are still two hours until the plane lands in Edinburgh, Scotland.

Scotland: a place my mother left when I was still a knuckle of cells hidden inside of her, small and secret. Somewhere there is a father that I've never met. A father who loved my mother for just long enough to make me.

I am not here for him.

I reach above me and turn the light back off. In the darkness of the plane, time smooths. I fall asleep with my head against the window, dark sky stretched out above and below me, and dream of incisors cracking bone, a flurry of fur, a scattering of spilled ash.

༜

Scotland is all heather-stark valleys, crumbled stone towers, and black lakes. I watch it through the windows of the train that takes me north out of Edinburgh. My mother had always told me that she met my father in the farthest away place she could find. When I asked her what he looked like, she said she couldn't remember his face. All she remembered was the sound of waves lapping against a shore and the smell of damp moss crushed under her feet.

There was a brief time, when I was seven or eight, when all I wanted was to know who my father was. My mom would get angry with me when I brought him up. "You're all mine," she'd say. "I dreamed about you for twenty-five years before you were born. All he did was shake you loose."

When the train reaches the end of its rails, I board another plane, smaller than the one I took to Edinburgh. It shudders over mountainsides painted with snow, then over the sea, and finally lands on an island called Shetland.

This is not the farthest away place I could find, but I hope it is close enough. When I leave the airport, it is nighttime and subfreezing. I like the way the cold makes me extra aware of my skin, goose-pimpled and electric. I climb into a cab, and the cold radiates off me, like it's my skin that's made of ice.

I have a hotel booked in a nearby town called Lerwick. My plan was to get some sleep, to shower off the miles I've traveled in the last twenty-four hours. In the morning I'd explore town. Maybe find a local to buy me a drink.

But as my cab gets into town, the driver's forced to a stop. The streets teem with people. Young and old, couples and families, gloved hands holding gloved hands, all walking in the same direction. I crane my neck to get a better look, but everyone's face is in shadow, or hidden under a hood, or wrapped under scarves.

"It's okay," I say to the driver. "I'll get out here."

I step out onto a street flanked by boxlike houses, gray or white and small-windowed. The sound of footsteps echoes flatly off them, but other than that, it's eerily quiet. I think of the warm hotel bed waiting for me just a couple blocks away and realize I'm not at all sleepy. I feel more awake than I've been for days, maybe weeks.

At the end of the street, the crowd gathers in a courtyard. They've begun forming a circle around a large bonfire, and as I get closer, I see there's a long, narrow ship in the center of the flames. On its prow: the carved face of a wolf, already blackened and half-chewed away by the blaze.

The crowd presses me closer to the fire until I can feel the heat against my cheeks. Someone's shoulder collides sharply with mine, and I stumble forward. When I find my balance, I'm surrounded by men in Viking helmets, torches gripped in their hands. They form a wall around the burning ship, separating it and the crowd, and I'm on the wrong side. The flames from their torches bend sideways in the wind. I smell scorching wood. My skin prickles with heat as the bottom of the ship gives out and the bonfire rears up.

Suddenly, someone grabs me by the shoulder and pulls me back into the crowd, away from the fire. I turn to thank the stranger, and I'm met with a man in a dark red cloak and a silver helmet. A torch is in his hand. He is tall and his hair is dark and long enough to stick out below his helmet. There's a small scar in the shape of an arrow on his jaw.

He takes a step back, stretching out his arms to make way for me to retreat farther from crowd's center.

But I don't. Not right away.

When my mother met a faceless stranger in a faraway place, she was not afraid.

I take his hand. His skin is warm and dry. His fingers close around mine.

I tell him, "My mother is dead. It was the old cliché, wrong place at the wrong time. Anyway, I was all hers, and now that she isn't here, I don't know what I am."

I pull back, and he looks at me. I'm not sure if he heard me over the blaze of the fire and the murmur of the crowd, but what's important is he doesn't say he's sorry. He's the only person I've told who hasn't said he's sorry.

At first, I am leading him, and then he is leading me. He leads me away from the fire to a gray building. He drops my hand as he fumbles beneath his cape, searching for something. He places his torch into a puddle by the front stoop, where it goes out in an instant and starts to smoke.

He unearths a key and unlocks the door and we walk through a hallway of doors until we reach the end, and then he takes me into his apartment. He doesn't turn on the lights, but the window blinds are open and the fire from the courtyard is enough to see by. I stand by the door as he removes his helmet and his armor, places them carefully, deliberately on the floor. I go to the window. "How far away is the sea?" I ask.

"Close enough to hear when there's a storm."

He pushes some clothes off the couch, and we sit down together. I think he will make a move, but we end up just watching the shadows move across the walls as the flames die in the courtyard.

"This night feels so long," I say.

He murmurs, sleepy, "In the winter in this city, it's almost always night."

I run my tongue along my teeth and feel for the sharp point. I lean over and place my teeth around the man's elbow resting on the back of the couch, but I don't bite down. I'm like a dog, just play fighting. Testing the boundary between hurt and play. I think about how strange it is that humans are one of the few animals that doesn't attack with teeth. The man looks at me, bemused, but doesn't push me away.

Beyond the window, the last flames go out. The room goes flat with darkness. If it wasn't for the sound of the man breathing next to me, I could pretend I was alone.

I feel around in the front pockets of my jeans for the lost piece of tooth, but I can't find it. I dig into the corners. I check my back pockets, though I already know it won't be there.

I get up. The man is asleep now, head lolling on the back of the couch. I gather my bags and step quietly toward the door. I imagine a part of me rolling across a train platform or snagging on a heather-choked hill or being washed down a gutter into a bay. I wonder if teeth, like hair, continue to grow after you're dead. I wonder if teeth are like seeds, and when they detach from your body, something inside of them clicks, they split open, and begin to grow roots.

Daughter

SHE ARRIVES in the middle of the night, a month early.

I wake to a cold sensation all over my stomach. The only thing I can compare it to is—you know the feeling—when you jump into a lake fed by snowmelt and your body goes all electric all at once and you feel a tug like your skin is trying to flee your skeleton. That's what it feels like, but only for a moment. Because before I even have time to wonder what is happening to me, my daughter is here. Emerging from my protruding belly. Actually, floating up through it.

She hovers over me, still in the fetal position. Sucking her thumb. Not aware yet that she's been born.

I stare at her, hardly breathing, like I'm afraid that my smallest movement will set something in motion. Something I'm not yet ready for. Her forehead is furrowed like a sweet old man's. She has eyelids, fingernails. She has two nostrils. She has ears! Her skin is shimmery and translucent. I can see straight through her to my toes at the end of the bed.

After a few minutes, or maybe it's only a few seconds, she starts to twitch. Her legs reach, the wrinkles on her knees folding in on themselves. Then she pauses, surprised by her range of movement. She opens her eyes—a miracle. Blinks. And then she screams. She screams like a flesh-and-blood baby. The sound slices through the walls.

I reach out to her for the first time. Holding her is like holding something in a dream. I'm doing it, but as soon as I think about it too much, she slips from my arms, bobs down the bed a little, and I need to reach for her again.

Even so, she seems comforted by my touch. Her eyes close. Holding her feels like holding thawing ice. The feeling of her melts down my arms. It's not unpleasant.

I remember, suddenly, that I should tell Luke.

Luke is traveling out of state this week for work. He was hesitant to leave, me being so pregnant, but we were supposed to have five more weeks. I told him to go.

I reach for my phone on the bedside table and snap a picture. My first selfie with my daughter. I try not to change my natural expression in any way. I want Luke to see me as I really am right now, in the afterglow of childbirth.

It's only after I send the picture that I notice how my daughter barely shows up against the flash of the camera. In the photo, she is hardly there.

Luke responds almost immediately with a shocked emoji. "Is she?" Luke texts.

"Not dead," I respond.

Then, an addendum. "But I think she might be a ghost." Minutes pass.

Then I get another text. "I'm coming home. Next flight available."

I place my phone back on the bedside table and notice in the sudden darkness that my daughter seems to emit a small amount of light. I close my eyes, and I can still see her there, her silhouette humming through my eyelids.

I must drift off, because when I open my eyes again, the curtains glow with the gray, early morning. I look for my daughter and find her hovering over the armoire, close to the ceiling. The sight of her so far off the ground sends a jolt of adrenaline through my chest, but she seems to be asleep, thumb tucked in her mouth like a mollusk in its shell. I stop myself from retrieving her. I don't want to become the sort of mother who prioritizes her own peace of mind over her daughter's independence, only six hours into motherhood.

My phone buzzes. I have fourteen missed texts from Luke. "I'm in Milwaukee!" he says. "All flights grounded due to snowstorm!" He sends a picture taken through the airport window of the runway covered in white, planes bursting from snowdrifts like icebergs, air traffic controllers making snow angels on one of the wings.

"How is she?" he asks.

"We're fine," I text Luke. And then I add, because I think it might make him feel good, "We miss you."

I feel something cool between my legs and reach under the blankets. Sometime in the night I must have passed the placenta, and with it the umbilical cord. I fish it all out from between my legs and clutch it in the hand that doesn't hold my phone.

Based on the dozens of birthing videos I watched while I was pregnant, I can tell they are not normal.

The placenta isn't goopy or bloody like I expected. It feels like cold silk. The umbilical cord seems to buzz under my fingers, like it's producing a very slight electrical current. I get this instinctive feeling that they, the placenta and the cord, must have magical properties. I put them in the drawer next to the bed, decide to worry about them later.

My phone buzzes again. "Have you been to the doctor?" Luke texts me. "Promise me you'll go to the hospital today."

I tell him I will. I promise.

I put my phone down and push back the blankets.

I don't want to get up, don't want to make the drive to the hospital. I put up with the pressing, the pricking, the poking, the fingers reaching inside me, the machines that turned my skin invisible, saw through straight to my organs. I put up with it all through my pregnancy because I told myself it would help the baby. But now that the baby is here, it feels impossible.

I remind myself that if, before, I was doing it for the baby, now, I'm doing it for Luke.

Luke, who missed his daughter's birth, who must be feeling so helpless right now and desperate to be involved. I can do this for him.

I get out of bed and teeter for a moment, unused to the new distribution of weight on my body.

I use a pregnancy magazine from the bedside table to fan my daughter out of the corner and out of the bedroom and toward the bathroom. I'm feeling proud of my ingenuity, until I accidentally pass her through a waste bin and she wakes up and starts screaming again. I leave the shower curtain open as I wash my hair so I can watch her as she howls, eyes screwed shut, translucent face turning a bright shade of pink.

"I know," I say to her. "I know."

I hum nothing tunes, trying to match them to the pitch of her screams.

In the waiting room at the doctor's office, there's a fish tank. It only contains one fish, an orange, bug-eyed goldfish. It hangs upside down just below the surface of the water. At first, I think it's dead, but its tail, its fins, still pump furiously. It swims little circles, scooping fish food flakes into its little, upside-down mouth. I can't keep my eyes off it.

The receptionist sees me watching.

"Swim bladder infection," he says. "The internet said to feed it peeled peas, but it didn't seem to work."

"Mrs. Scheerer," a woman calls from a doorway next to reception. "You and Baby are up."

I look away from the fish and follow her into the back, into a windowless room with a model cross section of a woman's uterus on the desk. The doctor is already waiting for us. He's a tall, scarecrow man with a red mustache and thick eyeglasses.

"Your obstetrician, Dr. Beal, isn't in the office today," he says, shaking my hand once, decisively, before letting it go. "But I hope I'll do just fine."

He indicates that I place my daughter on the exam table. I try, but she floats an inch above it, fists pumping, eyes blinking bewilderedly.

"Should I undress her?" I ask.

"Yes, please."

I hadn't been sure how to dress a ghost baby whose limbs seemed to slip out from under my fingers, so I'd wrapped her in a flannel blanket, tied it loosely with one of Luke's belts. I unclasp the belt now, let it and the blanket fall onto the table.

"Now, what do we have here?" The doctor peers over my daughter. He gets so close her tiny baby breaths fog up his glasses. Breath. That's something my baby has. "I've heard of this happening, but I've never seen it myself." He looks up at me, glasses slipped to the end of his nose. "Was it a normal pregnancy?"

I think about it, not sure what the honest answer would be.

Luke and I hadn't exactly meant to make a baby. For years we'd been deciding whether we wanted to be parents or not. Sometimes we'd come home from evenings at friends' houses, exhausted, stickers stuck in our hair, welts from airsoft pellets on our arms, and say, "Thank god we're never having kids." Other times, Luke and I would take a trip to the zoo and smile at the parents lifting their children up to touch noses with the polar bear through the glass, knowing that one day that would be us.

The problem was, I could truly imagine my life happy with or without a child. I was terrified by the responsibility of choice, and I think Luke felt the same. Eventually, we decided to let chance decide. I was thirty-eight years old. Luke was forty. We became careless with birth control, used it only occasionally. Only a couple of months into our experiment, my period was late. As I waited for one line or two lines to appear on the pregnancy test, Luke sat next to me.

When two lines appeared, Luke hugged me. "There's our answer," he said. And the way his eyes got glassy, the way his voice cracked, made me wonder if this was the outcome he'd hoped for all along.

During the next several months, I craved cold things.

Silky gelato.

Cool, freshly whipped cream with frozen blackberries.

Around month five, I stopped dreaming. In the morning, I'd have vague feelings of having spent the night floating in a pool of stars, or falling through an endless pit of snow.

Even though I was the one growing, I felt strangely disconnected from the pregnancy. Things happened without me making them happen. At my checkups, my doctor would announce that my baby had grown skin, a throat, a brain. So much growth without me having a say in it. Luke built a crib in the corner of the bedroom. Coworkers staggered into the office with grocery bags full of hand-me-down jumpers and cloth toys and teething necklaces. *Oh*, I'd think every time they showed up at my desk. *Those are for me. I'm the pregnant one.*

"It was as normal as a pregnancy can be, I guess," I say, finally, to the doctor.

He grunts, nods. He has a stethoscope hovered over my daughter's chest. He sighs. "Well, she has no vital signs that I can detect, but she doesn't seem bothered by that. What's her name?"

"Oh. She doesn't have one. My husband was traveling—he's stuck in an airport in Milwaukee. I think he'd be upset if I named her without him."

The doctor looks down at her, frowning. She does a couple of barrel rolls, midair, and spits up on the table. It doesn't look like regular, human spit. It's glittery and kind of pretty and dries up, or disappears, before I can wipe it away.

I pick up the blanket and wrap it back around my daughter. I hold her. She weighs nothing.

"So, what are the rules?" I ask. "How do I take care of her?"

"The rules," he repeats thoughtfully to himself. "Well, I'm sure you'll have to figure them out as you go along. But for now, I can tell you that she seems only partially incorporeal."

"Only partially?"

"Well, you managed to strap this blanket to her, and she's not falling through the exam table. But when I try to touch her, my finger goes straight through her skin. Like she's not there. I have a feeling she might be selectively corporeal." He chuckles. "Good luck keeping her from sneaking out through the walls when she's a teenager."

He gives me brochures and tells me to schedule a follow-up appointment for a week from now. As I walk with my daughter to the car, I flip through the brochure titles: *Readjust Your Expectations: When Mommyhood Isn't What You Expect*, *Simply Breastfeed!*, and *Hug Your Baby: The Importance of Skin to Skin*.

The parking lot is cold and coated in slush. In the corner of the lot, taking up three parking spots, is a mountain of snow mixed with gravel. I look down at my daughter. She blinks up at me, expressionless.

We arrive to a dark and quiet house. The first thing I do is flip on all the lights on the first floor, turn the thermostat up past seventy degrees, higher than I usually allow myself to set it.

I decide, for the first time, to try breastfeeding. I feel a pressure in my breast, but I'm not sure it's milk that I'm producing. What do ghosts eat? Energy? Memories? I arrange myself on the couch and lift my shirt. My daughter's mouth struggles to find my nipple, even with me guiding it to her lips. When she finally starts to suckle, I feel a tingly, pins-and-needles sensation spread across my chest. I feel a sinking in my stomach, like I'm falling.

My phone has not stopped dinging with messages from Luke. I'd sent him a text to tell him we went to the doctor's office, but that was over an hour ago. With one hand, I hold my daughter. With the other, I unlock my phone and scroll through the messages.

In Milwaukee, the snow hasn't stopped.

Luke says, "I'm afraid I'll be stuck in the airport overnight." Luke says, "How are you? How is the baby?"

Luke bought a bib that says "Wisconsin Is for Milk Lovers" in the airport gift shop. He sends me a picture of it around his neck, too small, choking him.

Luke wants to know if I want a shirt to match it.

Luke apologizes for not being with me. He apologizes again.

"Maybe I'll just rent a car and drive home. It's six hundred miles. I can be home by morning if I don't stop."

"Hello," Luke says. "Are you there?"

"Are you there?"

I know I should respond, put his mind at ease. But, for some reason, just the thought of typing out a message exhausts me. I turn my phone to silent, place it upside down on the arm of the chair.

As a rule, I try not to think negative thoughts about Luke. Growing up, I saw the women in my family, one by one, grow to despise their husbands. They loved them, maybe, but they didn't seem to like them anymore. At family gatherings, in the kitchen as we arranged gingerbread cookies on trays, in the backyard watching the little kids climb trees, they'd give me unasked-for advice. "Make sure you know who you're marrying before saying 'I do.'" "Keep a secret bank account." "If

he insists on you staying home and raising the kids, get a part-time job."
"Find someone who will take a lot of business trips and leave you the hell alone sometimes."

I tried to avoid the mistakes they claimed to have made. I dated carefully. I was with Luke for seven years before I agreed to marry him. Then I made up a rule for myself. That I'd focus on the positives. That I wouldn't live a life like my mother's and my aunts' and my grandmothers'. That I would be someone who was happy.

When my daughter finally falls asleep and detaches from my breast, I stand up and place her on the couch, where she floats an inch above the cushions.

I feel tired. Exhausted in a deep, existential way. Outside, the sun nods close to the horizon.

I decide it's time to start finding some answers to what my daughter might be.

I make myself chamomile tea. I open my laptop.

It doesn't take me long to find Reddit threads about mothers who have birthed ghosts. Some say a ghost child is a child born without a soul. Others say it's the result of a mother who hasn't found God. I find links to articles that say these ghost children are a real-life metaphor for our increased attachment to technology and our waning presence in the tactile world.

I leave these threads, annoyed. Where are the posts written by the mothers? Or by the ghost babies themselves, all grown up into ghost teenagers, ghost adults? Saying that everything is all right. That they've lived fulfilling lives with supportive parents. That it is actually pretty cool to be a ghost. Where are those articles? I wonder if maybe the doctor was right, that I'll have to figure it all out on my own as I go along.

I close my laptop and go to my daughter sleeping on the couch. I try to find the ways she looks like me, or the ways she looks like Luke, but she only looks like herself.

I kneel on the floor, lean close. Her breath on my cheeks is cold and faint. A draft moving through a room. A back door left open for too long. I turn my head to the side and lower my ear to her chest. I close my eyes. My head passes through her skin and lands where her rib cage should be. My ears crackle.

When I open my eyes, I expect to see the couch, or my arms, through the light glimmer of her translucent skin. Instead, I see darkness, broken up by small pinpricks of light. I inhale sharply and the darkness trembles. Splits open like a curtain. Behind it, I see my mother's face beaming down at me, wrinkles radiating around her eyes. The image distorts, contorts. I see my own hands, chubby and not yet grown, clutching a dead chick, its eyes bulging, feathers damp and clinging to its skin. Then it changes again. I see a broken cuckoo clock at my feet, my father in a doorway, just a silhouette.

I pull away. I pull away so hard I fall to my hands and knees, gasping. My face is damp, maybe from sweat, maybe from something else. I wipe it away with my knuckles.

When I'm able to sit back up, I realize my daughter's eyes have opened.

"I'm sorry," I begin to say to her, then stop. I stop because she's staring at me. She's staring at me like she knows me. Not just me as her mother, the person who carried her for eight months. She sees me. My secrets. My vices. Every time I slipped and let my love for Luke be momentarily replaced with revulsion. My failures. Memories I thought weren't memories anymore, long forgotten.

I pick her up. She must want me to pick her up, because she doesn't fall through my hands.

I ask, "Who are you?"

※

That night, it starts to snow. The snow falls so heavily I can hear it hitting the screens in the windows. I can hear it piling on the bird feeder in the backyard.

I've barely eaten all day, so I decide to make a meal. Something decadent that will require multiple steps. I settle on a lasagna.

I place my daughter over the sink, which I've filled with hot water and soap to soak the dishes once I'm done with them. She bats happily at the bubbles and peaks of foam that form on the surface of the water. I brown ground meat in the pan. Dice onion and garlic on the wooden cutting board. I don't have tomato paste, so I take overripe tomatoes from the counter and pulp them in a bowl with my bare hands. It feels good to spend so much time making something that only I will enjoy.

As I cook, I talk to my daughter.

I tell her I once read an article about a species of crab that lives hundreds of feet beneath the ocean's surface. As an adult, this crab has a maximum leg span of almost four meters. But as a baby, it's transparent and round and legless. It floats on the surface of the water like plankton.

I tell her that the ocean is full of creatures that are transparent, just like her.

I tell her about the time I was almost pulled out to sea and drowned by a rogue current. I was in my early twenties and had driven eight hours to the coast by myself. At first, I wasn't scared. Watching the beach recede, farther and farther away, I felt buoyant and excited. It didn't occur to me until I saw the lifeguard, now small and featureless in the distance, waving an orange preserver, that I should be fighting the current.

My daughter doesn't look at me, just keeps playing with the soap bubbles. But still, I think she's listening.

After dinner, I wrap her in blankets and put on my boots and walk out into the front yard, where the snow has piled so high that I can no longer tell where my yard ends and the road begins. There's no one out walking their dogs, no one driving. It's just the two of us.

"Snow," I say to my daughter. "This is snow."

The cold doesn't seem to bother her. She leans into the crook of my arm, yawns. The shape her mouth makes, her little tongue. It's all so perfect it feels painful.

I wonder if this is the same snow that falls six hundred miles away in Milwaukee. Or if we are showered by our own personal snow cloud. I imagine a future in which the snow keeps falling and falling. It forms a mountain between me and my husband. He's safe where he is. But he can't reach us.

I suddenly remember the umbilical cord that I placed in the drawer this morning. Still holding my daughter in my arms, I run upstairs, retrieve it, and then return to the front yard.

Again, I get the feeling that it is something magical. "What does this do?" I ask my daughter.

I swing it. I rub it between my fingers and try to make a wish. I toss it in the snow. It does nothing that a regular umbilical cord wouldn't do, apart from emitting a soft glow.

I pick the cord back up, and this time my daughter reaches for it. In her hands, the cord begins to buzz. Just a little. Then, it begins to tug.

It pulls upward, like it's attached to a giant, invisible balloon. I let go, startled. But my daughter holds on.

She rises from my arms and I grasp for her. Her skin is like silk and I can't get a grip. She doesn't want to be held, and so she becomes unholdable. She slips out from under the blankets. She rises until she's just out of my reach and then goes higher.

I didn't even get the chance to name her, I think reflexively.

I wonder if I can run into the house and up to the second-story window, trying to catch her from there. But it's too late. She's already cleared the roof.

My daughter floats up into the dark, starless sky. I can see the bottoms of her feet. She's kicking and kicking. Joyfully, I realize. I can hear her laugh, her very first laugh, loud and unrestrained, drifting down with the snow. She stops rising and starts floating to the west, in the direction of the set sun.

The front door is still open, the lamp from the foyer casting a bright box around me in the snow. Somewhere inside the house, my phone lights up with messages from far away. A half-eaten lasagna cools on a plate.

I leave it.

I leave it all.

I run after my daughter. I follow the sound of her laughter. As I run, snow kicking up behind me, I start laughing, too. I see faces appearing in windows, fingers splitting blinds open to peer out at me. I smile at them and just keep running. I've never run so fast in my life, my daughter as my guide.

Body Doubles

IN THIS TOWN, humans shed their skin like reptiles. The streets and parks and cul-de-sacs and ice cream shops and bank lobbies teem with our translucent doubles. They somersault in the winds, get caught in windshield wipers when it rains, drift into the river and get tangled in the motors of speed boats or pulled up in crawdad traps. Those of us who bike to work complain about them getting caught in our bike spokes.

It's a damn nuisance.

But it hasn't always been this way.

We remember a time, though it's been years now, when folks in our town dropped skin the normal way. Microscopic dead skin cells that we never missed. Skin that would turn into dust and carpet the top shelves of bookcases.

Some say the shedding started with an experimental skin care product meant to rid your skin of acne scars. There is a factory upriver that produces lotions and scrubs and cleansers. Maybe a pipeline cracked. Maybe a crooked manager dumped waste over the bank in the dead of night. Either way, one theory is that the chemicals seeped into the watershed, and to this day we poison ourselves with every sip of water from the tap.

Others say it was our fault. That we brought it on ourselves psychosomatically. We toiled too long, not talking about our lived and inherited traumas. Now, our bodies have had enough and are releasing the unspoken secrets through our skin, like toxins sweat out in a sauna.

It's true that many of our histories contain darkness. Family secrets come out after someone dies and the daughters begin digging through basements, or when a grandkid gets inspired to do a family tree project and starts sifting through the archived newspapers at the local library. Secrets brooding in the corners of our homes, guiding the trajectory of our lives. But who has the time or energy to dwell on all that? We're a town of farmers, of diner owners, of factory workers, of wall builders. We're the children of miners, before the mines were sealed shut. We have lives that keep us on our feet, or in the sun, or with our hands wrist-deep in dirt.

At first, we thought our doubles were kind of special. They have a sort of holographic, rainbow glimmer when held up to light in the right way. The skins keep their shape if we're careful, but crumple as easy as paper lanterns.

Adults shed every few months to a year. We know it's coming when we feel ticklish for no reason. Or when we stay awake all night staring at the ceiling, but don't feel tired in the morning. We step out of our old skin, and our new skin is younger than the one we've left behind. No more bug bites. No more cesarian scar. No more bruise.

Kids shed the most often. After school, dozens of translucent child-doubles roam the playground like a herd of deer at dusk, before the Clean Team has time to vacuum them up and dispose of them in the dumpster.

Some of the kids get attached to their doubles, which is kind of cute at first. They tie them to their wrists with a piece of string and fly them in the backyard like kites. They give them names and call them friends. They set plates for them at dinner time and tip empty cups to their paper-thin lips. If their parents try to throw the doubles away, they cry like their parents have abandoned *them*, their real, flesh children. But then, a few weeks later, they shed a new skin. A new self to befriend. And they forget their pain.

We feel like we've lived with the doubles long enough to know everything about them. That is, until Kaylee goes missing.

Kaylee is seven years old, young for a third grader, when her mother finds a hollow, daughter-shaped shell under the sheets instead of her daughter. At first, the mother thinks Kaylee must have shed in her sleep and, frightened by the unexpected ghostly copy of herself in bed, ran away and hid. Kaylee was a sensitive child, apt to cry under her desk during tests at school. But the mother can't find her anywhere. Not in her closet, not in the laundry hamper, not under the raspberry bush in the backyard.

Then, the next day, Miles disappears, as well. His father finds his double curled up on his beanbag chair. And then there's Leah, then Shubham. Every day, another child vanishes in their sleep, leaving only their shed skin behind.

We're in hysterics. We stop sleeping. We link arms and move through the woods, flushing out deer, chasing groundhogs from their holes, not leaving a single inch unsearched. We dredge the river. We buy drones with night vision cameras, so when it becomes too dark to search, we can fly them around town, peering into our neighbors' windows. There are so many drones in the sky, they sometimes crash into each other. We're not very good at piloting them yet, though we're getting better.

The parents of the lost children keep their doubles. They sit their hollow children at the kitchen table during dinner, arrange them in bed at night, sit them in front of the television and put on their favorite cartoons and let the TV play all day long. The parents discover if they turn on the ceiling fan at full speed, the doubles move a little bit, like they're breathing.

After a while, we start to wonder if there was something to the children's attachment to these doubles. What if these doubles aren't just hollow skins? What if they still contain something essentially *us*?

A month passes. Every day or so another kid disappears, until only the teenagers are left. Not a single child has been recovered, and our hopes of ever finding them wane. We begin spending more time with the doubles. After a few are accidentally crushed by well-meaning hug-gers—their hollow bodies so fragile, so easily broken—the parents set up permanent homes for them. The parents build thrones out of plywood, spray paint them black or neon green or lavender, the children's favorite colors. They surround them with toys. With Tamagotchi, with Pokémon cards, with fidget spinners, with snap bracelets, with fairies that spin and fly when you pull a string. All the toys their sons and daughters put on their Christmas lists that were deemed too expensive or too trivial at the time. They get those toys now.

The parents start missing work. They miss Sunday mass. They miss book club. When we stop by their homes with casseroles or pies or bouquets of flowers, we find them sitting at their children's altars. Their eyes are bloodshot and their hair is dull. We wonder when they've last shed their skin.

Join us, they say. So, we do.

Together, we bow our heads in front of the translucent children. We get to our knees.

The children look down on us with smooth, blank eyes.

At first, we don't know what to say. We tell them we miss them. We tell them about the ice hockey game they missed last week, or about the red-tailed hawk we saw snatch a finch clean out of the sky.

And then, presently, we start to whisper our secrets. We tell them everything, and when we run out of things to tell, we share every dark thought, every ill wish. Every suspicion about ourselves we worry is true.

The children's doubles nod in an invisible breeze, and we think we can see a blush of pink in their cheeks, just maybe. We ask them to please, please forgive us.

At the End of the Tunnel

IN THE MINES, I am alone.

In the old days, before I was born, men would carry canaries in cages underground with them. But I'm not a man, and I don't have a canary, and I wouldn't want one anyway, because a canary would drown out the sounds of the tunnels.

A tunnel sounds like the beginning of a yawn.

A tunnel sounds like a ghost in the cupboard.

I go into the mines on rainy days, on snowy days, on days when fog blankets my valley town. Days when the wet smell of the forest seeps through the cracks in the house where I live by myself, and I get this feeling like I want to burrow. In the mines, I wear a headlamp and carry a backpack filled with matches, a canteen of water, apples, a ball of yarn, and five little glass jars to hold any treasures I find: a bat skull, a rusted belt buckle, an empty snail shell. I can spend an entire day there and never feel lonely or afraid.

In the old days, men descended into the mines and picked at the walls for copper, for iron, for knuckle-sized nuggets of coal. They dug so deep that the air grew heavy and warm and then they dug deeper, following the veins of ore. But eventually, the walls stopped glittering. The ore ran out. They abandoned their mines, leaving behind wooden minecarts on steel rails to rot, lanterns with panes of glass that crack like ice under my feet, lunch pails with initials scratched on the bottom. Little clues for me to piece together what the mines held before they held me.

In my regular life, I work at a grocery store. When my coworkers ask why I come in on Monday with scabbed over knuckles or red dirt on my shoes, I tell them I'm a recreational rock climber. But then they want to know where I climb. They want to know what equipment I use. Why do people always have so many questions? Sometimes I think they're just asking to be polite and sometimes I think they sense I have a secret life that they're trying to uncover. I challenge myself to see how long I can go without speaking. I make sure the shelves have enough cartons of eggs, sacks of flower, white mushroom caps. I move the ripe avocados to the top of the pile. I build towers of Granny Smiths. I answer questions in smiles and gestures. I don't say a word.

Every couple of weeks, after work, I get dinner with a group of women I've known since we were children. They're all married with babies at home. We always meet at the same restaurant, a diner where you can order both pancakes and whiskey at any time of the day. Around them, I never have to talk about myself. Their lives seem fraught with drama. Their husbands make unwise investments and have affairs with coworkers. Their children set fires in their backyards and release goldfish into the neighbors' pools.

When their attention does land on me, it's to ask when I'll marry. They don't really expect an answer. They turn to each other before I can take a breath, say how perfect it would be if I could find a nice farmer, or a woodsman. A man with strong hands and a collection of bearskins to keep me warm when the snow comes. If they waited long enough, I know what I'd say. I'd tell my friends I'm too busy to date, because that'd be easier than explaining that I prefer mines to men.

I did date a few times, years ago. I dated, because, like moving out of my parents' house, like finding a job, it seemed like the thing I was supposed to do at that point in my life. I dated all sorts of people. A man who practiced falconry. A man who could dance his fingers along the neck of a fiddle so quickly I swore he was made of flickering flames instead of flesh and bone. I dated a woman who could sing dragonflies into her palm. I dated another who could shoot a squirrel out of a tree from a hundred yards away. But they never excited me like walking into the woods did, or like exploring the cave eventually did. My dates hugged me, and I felt bored. They reached for my hand, and I felt my chest constricting. As soon as I met them, I was waiting for them to leave again.

Once, one of my dates asked me why I never talked about myself. "What are you so afraid of me knowing?" she asked teasingly, leaning forward over the table that separated us, candlelight splashing new contours onto her face. "What's the harm in telling me what you're thinking right now?"

No one had ever asked me that question before, and the answer felt so obvious that I was surprised she hadn't already figured it out on her own. The harm in telling her about myself was that if I opened a little, she would want more and more. Ever since I was a girl, I'd sensed my desires and needs were different from other people's. I didn't know how to make myself understandable to others. I didn't want to have to.

She never asked to see me again, and I never asked to see her. It was only a few months later that I found the mines. Barely three miles from my home, in the thick woods behind my house. Concealed behind a blackberry bush. An empty doorway propped up by metal beams. I stepped cautiously through the entrance. Dead leaves carpeted the ground. A snake skin brushed against my ankle. I walked, chin tucked against my chest to avoid hitting my head on the low ceiling, until there was no longer light to guide me. Then, I sat. The earth was cool beneath my thighs. I breathed in the smell of the warm, damp air. Let it fill me up. Let my consciousness stretch away from my own body, into the corners of the tunnel, to the slow, steady drip of moisture.

A sharp cracking sound jolted me back into myself.

I got to my feet.

"Hello," I called, and my voice echoed. My voice magnified, repeating itself in the dark.

Maybe teenagers already occupied these mines, using the tunnels to smoke pot or drink out of sight of their parents. But when no one responded, my mind went to a story I hadn't thought about in years. Miners used to believe they shared their tunnels with Knockers: little, humanoid creatures with long, white beards and wrinkly faces. When I was a girl, my father, whose own father had worked in coal mines in a different town many years before, told me bedtime stories about men wandering underground for days, disoriented, following the sound of footsteps they could never catch up to. The Knockers could be benevolent or devious. Sometimes they'd tap on the walls to warn miners that a tunnel was about to collapse. Other times they'd snatch the canaries from their cages and blow out the miners' candles so they'd get lost in the dark.

I used to think they that the miners in my father's tales were just superstitious. But, underground, I find myself believing in things I normally don't.

Underground, I believe in monsters that live deep, deep in the earth until someone wakes them up. I believe in ghosts.

The next week, I returned to the mines. And I kept coming back. In the mines, that tight feeling in my chest disappears. I can go hours without uttering a single word. Time disappears. I feel wiped free of anything that plagues me above ground.

Sometimes I get this feeling that it wasn't men who built these mines, but me. Past versions of myself. I imagine that I must have been reincarnated dozens of times, each time finding my way to these tunnels. I find a footprint encased in long-dried mud and when I hover my own foot above the print, they're the same size. Then, I find a rusty pickaxe with a grip that fits my hand perfectly. A few days later, I trip over a helmet, and when I try it on, it's snug without being too tight. Like it was made for me. I start carrying the pickaxe and wearing the helmet every time I go underground.

One spring morning, almost a year after I first entered the mines, I find a tunnel that branches off from a route I'd walked many times before. The entrance to the new tunnel is narrow, set against an outcropping of rock usually hidden in the shadow my headlamp casts against the walls. But on this day, the light hit the walls differently. I see the entrance where before I'd only seen darkness.

I can tell immediately that this tunnel is alive. I learned to tell the difference between a tunnel that was alive and one that was dead soon after I started exploring the mines. Most tunnels are dead. In dead tunnels, nothing changes other than the occasional rock breaking loose from the wall or a rat decomposing in a corner. Everything is perfectly preserved, the air dry and static. But living tunnels are connected to veins of water that kept them growing. Calcium salt drips from the ceilings. Drops of water hang, suspended, from the end of stalactites like jewels on the ears of a woman.

I enter, wondering how many times I've walked it in the past, thinking I knew my surroundings, thinking I understood the mines, not seeing what was right in front of me. The new tunnel is so narrow I need to walk sideways, leading with my shoulder. I stop to catch my breath. When I inhale, my chest presses against the wall, so I feel like I can't take a full breath. I shine my light ahead, hoping to make out where the tunnel widens, but I can't see more than a few yards ahead before the path curves out of sight.

For the first time in the mines, I feel truly afraid.

I get that feeling I did when I was a child, playing hide and seek in my parents' bedroom closet. Normally I wasn't allowed in their closet. I let my hands float over rows of fabric in the dark, finding clothing I'd never seen them wear. A wedding dress wrapped in plastic. Pointed, impossibly tall heels. A folder full of letters addressed with names I didn't recognize. A locked box. I had the feeling that if I stayed, if I looked too hard, I'd find more than I wanted to know. I'd learn truths about my parents that I could never unlearn.

I stopped the game. I left.

I do the same now. I back up out of the tunnel quickly enough that I scrape my hand on the walls. I leave blood on the rocks.

I stride out of the mines and back to my home, where I lock the door. I don't understand why I'm shaking.

That week, when I meet up with the women at the diner, I can't even pretend to listen to their stories. My mind is underground, trying to see past the darkness in the narrow tunnel. When one of them says, "I know someone who you might like," I answer, "Sure," without fully hearing what she's saying.

"Perfect," she says. "I'll arrange everything. Tomorrow night, okay?"

I nod, deciding I'll cancel last minute anyway. But when the next day comes, I feel like I need a distraction from thinking about the mines.

I meet the man at a tavern in town. I wear jeans and a T-shirt, refusing to make a special effort for a stranger. He wears work boots and a flannel shirt. He is a large man, with a coiled, brown beard and thick thighs and strong hands, the kind of man my friends married or wished they'd married.

He buys a pitcher of ale and pours us each a glass.

"So, what do you do?" he asks me. "In your free time? What do you enjoy?"

I shrug. "I like being outside. I like walking."

He nodded. "That's good. Me too. So do I."

He reaches across the table, and without giving me the chance to pull away, takes my hands in his, rubs his thumb along the scabs that have formed on my skin. Then he looks at me and chuckles, something in my expression apparently making him laugh.

"This makes you nervous, doesn't it?" he says, smiling.

I don't answer. The truth is, holding his hands feels no different than holding a sun-warmed stone, or a pitcher of water, or a pot of tea.

"It's okay," he says. "It's cute. I don't meet many shy girls anymore."

I pull away, and he lets me, but he keeps his eyes stuck on mine. His expression gets serious. "Who hurt you, honey?"

The question startles me. "No one," I say.

He smiled gently. "Everybody's been hurt by somebody. But you can't let yourself stay broken forever. Your friends told me how long it's been since you've had love. No one stays alone for so long unless they've been wounded."

I stand. I take a step backwards. "I'm going. I—I feel like going now."

"Don't run away, hon," he says, but I am already on my way out the door.

Back at home, I decide I'm not going to wait another day. Tomorrow I'll return to the mines. I'd rather face whatever lies in that tunnel then lead the rest of my days with people who tell me I'm broken.

That next morning, I leave my house earlier than usual. I pull on my dusty boots, my jeans, and my helmet. I fill my backpack with scones and a thermos full of coffee to drink on the way. Then I step outside into my yard facing the woods. The valley is awash with fog, the world gray in the early light. Trees, boulders, and bushes fade in and out of focus like passing ghosts.

It takes me less than an hour to reach the mines, and it's a relief to enter their stillness. It only takes me fifteen more minutes to reach the narrow tunnel.

The air is heavy and moist, like I remember it. I can feel the moisture beading on my upper lip. The passage is narrow, and I'm forced into a crab-walk. When I feel my heart start to thump in my chest, I slow my breaths. I focus only on forward movement. I pay so much attention to not tripping over the small, twisted stalagmites that seem to burst from the ground like horns, that I don't realize I've reached the end of the tunnel until I collide with it.

I gasp a little and take a few steps backwards.

In front of me is a door.

About five feet tall, three feet wide. Built out of dark wood. I trace my light along its frame, find metal hinges and a tarnished, bronze doorknob.

I put my ear to it. The wood is soft, gives a little as I press into it, like it's rotten in the middle. I close my eyes and listen. I am painfully aware of the sounds of my own body. The air filling my chest cavity, then rushing out through my nostrils. My stomach growling as the muscles contract around the empty space. I hold my breath, close my eyes, try to still my body for a moment, just long enough to listen.

I hear a tap.

The tap is clear, staccato. I call it a tap, because I don't want to call it a knock. A knock has a Knocker.

I open my eyes, step back, and drop to my knees. My breath is coming too quickly. I feel my heart pounding in my temples.

I want to disappear.

I reach up, switch off my headlamp. Become invisible.

If I turn back now, I know I'll never come back to the mines. I'll have to spend the rest of my life pretending to be something understandable, something able to be put into words.

I stand. Make myself big. Switch my headlamp back on.

I place my hand on the doorknob to steady myself. The metal is cool and sweaty in my palm.

I turn the knob.

And nothing happens. It's locked. Or maybe it's been rusted shut. Maybe over years of disuse, the cave has grown around it, like a tree trunk growing around a chain link fence.

I think about how as still as the earth may seem, it is always moving. Its movements measured in millennia instead of moments. Once upon a time, this tunnel might have had a different entrance, one that has closed up in the time since. Am I on the outside of the door, or am I inside?

I curl my fingers into a fist, and the scabs on my hands crack, maybe start to bleed. I knock twice on the door.

I wait.

Then, something knocks back.

I know it's a knock this time. Not a tap.

Two knocks, the sound of something alive.

My heart is galloping. I could turn around now. I could close this tunnel with a wall of rocks, I could leave the mines forever. I could turn away from this mystery. But I am not broken. There is nothing wounded about me. I built these mines. I dug deeper into the earth than anyone before me, and then I kept digging. I've died in these mines, was lost and starved, inhaled gas seeping silently from between the rocks, was crushed in a rockfall. But then I was reborn.

I take the pickaxe from my belt. The handle is warm under my fingers. So much warmer than the man's hands in the tavern. I hold the pickaxe high over my head. I aim for the door. I swing.

The door splinters. It doesn't give.

I raise the axe again.

Swing.

This time it breaks through, puts a fist-sized hole in the wood.

I think about stopping. Peering through the split in the wood, shining my light on whatever lies on the other side from the safety of this side of the door. But now that I've started on this path, I can't slow myself down. I let my pickaxe drop to my side. I raise my leg, knee bent, and I kick. Is this what it was like for my friends when they fell in love? Was it like fighting their way through a dark tunnel, their feet and hands moving them forward almost against their will? I kick and kick at the already weakened door until it collapses, soft and rotten, at my feet.

Ahead of me is more tunnel. I step through the now empty door-frame. I swing my light along the rocky walls. They're damp, flesh-like, covered in waxy formations that look slimy to the touch. I feel like I'm crawling through the body of a giant beast.

I swing my light into the pitch blackness ahead of me, and the beam wraps around a figure. A humanoid.

I gasp and step backwards, but I keep my light trained on the being. Its back is to me. It's wearing dusty brown overalls. I can't tell how tall it is, because it is bent over, like it's picking something up off the floor. A pickaxe like mine swings from its left hand.

I think now that the Knockers from the stories must be real. I try to remember if there was a way to gain the Knockers' favor. If they can be won over by gold or bread or a good riddle. As the figure in front of me begins to stand and turn, I wish silently for a good Knocker. One of the Knockers that warns of cave-ins, that leads lost miners back to the light, that finds gems in the deep belly of the earth and shares its wealth with those it meets.

It's facing me now, and I can't understand what I'm looking at. The figure is as tall as I am. It doesn't have a long, white beard. It doesn't have a gnarled, wrinkly face.

It has my face.

She has my face.

Her hair is longer than mine, and she's much paler. But she has my long nose, my slightly droopy left eyelid, my downturned mouth.

She walks up to me. Slowly. Dragging the pickaxe behind her so that it draws a line in the dirt. When she's only a few feet away, she drops the pickaxe at her feet and reaches out to me with her free hands. When we touch, I feel electrified. The hair on my arms stands up. She grips my forearms, her fingers pressing into the flesh, her skin as cool as the underside of a stone.

I realize I'm not afraid. I'm feeling something more complicated, something older than fear.

With one of her hands, she reaches up, and before I can stop her, switches off my headlamp. I prepare to plunge into darkness. But the cave doesn't go dark. Instead, everything around me glimmers silver, like a desert under a full moon.

I look at her, her with my face. In this strange cave-light, her eyes look purple. I know mine must be, too.

"Are you a Knocker?" I ask. Her lips twitch. I think it's a smile. "Am I Knocker?" I ask.

I get the feeling I'm not asking the right questions. Her fingers stay wrapped around my arms, but it doesn't feel like she's trying to restrain me. The pressure of her fingers on my arms feels safe, safe like the hug of the tunnel around us, safe like the slow and steady growth of stalactites.

I dig my heels into the dusty ground. I think of a new question. "Can I stay?"

This time she smiles for real. Full teeth. Crooked in the same places mine are. She lets go of my arms and turns and I follow her. I follow her as the tunnel slopes down, and the tunnel widens. I feel like I'm on my way somewhere.

❦

I don't remember eating or sleeping, and yet I never feel hungry or tired. I sense that I have been here for a very, very long time.

Every now and then I catch a memory of my past. A little house by the woods. Parents scolding me for saying the wrong thing. I know these memories are real, but it's like memories of a dream. They don't matter.

There are more than two of us now. We all look like sisters, nearly identical. Small things make us different. The number of teeth in our mouths, the length of our hair. The pattern of moles on our arms. One of us looks like she might have been a queen. She wears her hair in a braid nested around the top of her head. Another looks like she was a fighter. A knight. Her biceps large and round enough to fill our palms. Her hair shaved close to her skull.

We travel through the earth in a line, occasionally tapping on the walls of the tunnels to remind each other we're there.

When a tunnel ends, we pick up our pickaxes, and we form new tunnels.

We riddle the earth full of holes.

The earth creaking around us is a language I can understand.

My Ulcer

THERE'S AN ULCER in my stomach. I wake up with the knowledge that I have waited too long, postponed going to the doctor for too many Mondays, and now it's begun chewing a hole through my stomach and into some other part of my body. I know this like I know my name. Part of me is relieved to finally know the truth about my ulcer. For months I've suspected that it was there, suspected its desire to break free of my stomach, even when my friends told me I just needed to drink less soda, even when my mother told me people in my family didn't get ulcers and if I could only relax I'd feel better. Now that I know that I was right about it all along, I feel calm in a way I haven't in a very long time. I have an ulcer! It explains so much. On the way to the bathroom, I pass my roommate, her hair wet, tied up in a towel. "I have an ulcer!" I announce. "Oh no," she says, but she doesn't diverge from her path to her bedroom. I can tell she's bored with me. She's used to me announcing my ailments in the morning. I wish I could communicate to her that this time is different. Everything will be different from now on. I start my day, giddy with this new knowledge of myself. I am a person with an ulcer now. I wash my face and get dressed and take the elevator to the ground floor and walk to the corner pharmacy. I go to the Digestive Health section. I grab the largest bottles of probiotics, of antacids, of slippery elm capsules, of Herbal Stomach Repair by Lily of the Desert. Then I walk to the market and buy white rice, kale, blueberries, wheatgerm, and cabbage juice, foods that Google tells me are useful in the treatment of ulcers. My life will revolve around the care of this ulcer. I feel so lucky. Most people go their whole lives not understanding why they feel depressed in the afternoons, or why one out of five days they hate work with a ferocity that frightens them, or why sometimes they're sitting at a table with their best friends and realize they couldn't care less if they all got trapped in a cave tomorrow and were never seen again. If I ever feel any of these things in the future, I'll know that it's just because of the ulcer and I'll pop a slippery elm supplement. Or I'll make a blueberry smoothie. When I get home from the market, my roommate is in the kitchen, making a sandwich with her back to me. She's swaying her hips, and I can see earbuds tucked under her hair. It makes me sad to see her here alone, listening to music through headphones when she could be playing it out loud. I always thought of my roommate as a happy person, but now I wonder if she, too, harbors a quiet disease. A virus hidden where no one can see it. I walk past her unnoticed and go to my room. Alone, I lie down on my bed and roll up my shirt. I place a hand on my stomach. I try to locate where the ulcer is now. Has it reached my ribs yet? Has it reached my heart? Soon I'll be a body riddled with tunnels that my ulcer has carved. My body will contain a maze that's always becoming more complicated, full of dead ends that always have the potential to connect again.

The Sanctuary

SATURDAY IS MEDICAL DAY at Happy Bellies: Potbelly Pig Rescue and Sanctuary.

I see the veterinarian coming from miles away, a smudge of brown dust to the west. He's late, probably got lost on the winding backroads that lead from here to the interstate. I wipe sweat off my upper lip with the back of my hand and lock up the pen where I've spent all morning lathering sunscreen onto the pigs' backs and the tips of their ears. I pull my Happy Bellies baseball cap down over my forehead. Nine o'clock and already the heat blisters across the desert. The world flattens under its weight.

I reach the parking lot at the same time as the vet. I can tell he's never been here before by the way he carefully maneuvers around the potholes and doesn't know to park in the shade of the mesquite tree. It'll be over a hundred and thirty degrees in his car by the time he leaves.

"It's beautiful out here," he says, shielding his eyes as he steps out of the car.

That's what everyone says the first time they see the desert. And although it's true that it's beautiful, I've learned that what they really mean is: *Why would anyone choose this place to build a pig sanctuary?* When it storms, flash floods muscle over the washes and onto the roads, trapping the staff on an island of pigs. In the hottest months we drive an hour south to Tucson twice a day, sometimes three times, to stock up on potable water. We can drain two thousand gallons in under twelve hours. In July and August, we chill towers of wet towels in our industrial-sized freezers and drape them over the pigs' backs so nobody overheats.

"Thomas," he says, extending his hand.

His fingers envelop mine. He's tall enough that I need to squint up at his face and cup my eyes with my free hand. He's much younger than the last vet who came out here to work with us, but still older than me. He has thick eyebrows and brown eyes and long hair knotted at the nape of his neck. But the most noticeable thing is his mouth which seems too big for his face. It droops down at the corners like it might slide off.

I release his hand.

"You can set up in here," I say, and show him into the small ranch house that we've repurposed into a visitor center and clinic. He rolls a large, black case behind him. It makes me think of a magician's kit, and I try not to stare at it as I wonder what it might contain.

"Sorry about all this," I say, waving at the boxes of souvenir T-shirts and outdated pig-themed calendars and piles of neatly folded comforters donated by guests for when the weather turns cold. "The clinic space is in the back."

I leave him flipping through a box of potbelly pig magnets as I go to fetch one of my favorite pigs from her pen. Lucy. We noticed the drag in her belly a few days ago. Most of the pigs we need to perform abortions on are new to the Sanctuary. Before we introduce a pig to the others, we always make sure they are spayed or neutered. But we've had Lucy for a few weeks now. Somehow, she must have slipped through the cracks in the system, such as it is.

Lucy smells like maple syrup. Petting her is like petting a hairy boulder. A single fang protrudes from under her top lip. Her eyes are almost completely hidden under rolls of forehead fat, and her neck wobbles as she hoofs toward me. Lucy is my favorite, because I am her favorite. She's possibly the ugliest pig in our care, but she doesn't know it. She's the quickest to roll onto her back for a belly rub, and when I'm doing my rounds, she'll follow me at my heels like a puppy.

I don't need to leash her like I would the other pigs. Lucy stays at my side as I guide her to the clinic, where Thomas has already set up an ultrasound machine. I pet Lucy's snout and scratch at the thick skin between her ears as he holds the probe under her belly.

The screen beside us shows indistinct shapes, all black and white. "Potbelly pigs don't develop skeletons until the end of their first month," Thomas says. "That's how we'll know how far along she is. If the fetuses haven't formed skeletons yet, they'll be reabsorbed into her body."

"And if not?"

"They'll mummify," he says, not looking at me. "And things will be more complicated."

He holds the detector gingerly against Lucy's belly and rests one hand on her side, barely touching her. I want to tell him he doesn't have to be so gentle. I want to tell him that pigs, even pregnant pigs, are as tough as you'd expect them to be. I imagine Thomas with a boneless fetus cupped in the palms of his hands, pink and amorphous, a clenched fist of cells. Minutes pass. He clears his throat.

"Sorry," he says. "This is my first time. Doing this by myself, I mean. Oh, here we are." He points to the sonogram with his free hand. "Four, five, six... Seven babies. No indication of skeletal development." He grins at me, and I wonder if he'll give me a thumbs up.

I turn to the screen and try to see what he sees, but looking at the sonogram is like watching fish move beneath thick ice. The veterinarian we had before Thomas had preferred to work alone, always waved us out of the room if we lingered. This is the first time in two years that I've seen a sonogram. Looking at it makes my throat constrict, like it's fighting to keep something out.

Thomas pulls a syringe from his case, and I press my forehead to Lucy's damp snout so I don't see the needle go in. I feel Lucy's wet, warm maple breath mix with my own.

"All done," he says. "Wasn't that easy?" Like it was me he had injected.

He stuffs a hand into his pocket, wrestles out his wallet, and passes me a business card. It's slightly crumpled at the corners. "I'll be in next Saturday," he says. "Call me if you need anything sooner?"

I take the card without really feeling it and stick it into the back pocket of my shorts.

I think of the drugs moving through Lucy's veins, starting a chain reaction. A monsoon flood stripping the desert bare.

⁂

I grew up in Mesa, seventy miles from Happy Bellies, but some mornings I wake up feeling like I'm in a foreign country. Before coming here, I'd never seen a hawk talon a smaller bird from the air. I'd never seen a bat cling to a saguaro bloom. I'd never seen a shrike impale a lizard on the spines of a barrel cactus. I grew up amongst palm trees and sprinklers. I grew up smashing scorpions with frying pans and shooing grackles from the hoods of cars in the Circle K parking lot. The only times I ever went into the desert were in high school, when friends and I would drive into the Superstitions at sunset, fast on the winding back roads, windows down, jackrabbits fleeing from the high beams, or when, in summer, we'd float down the Salt River with coolers of beer tied to our innertubes and we'd let our skin burn until it peeled.

I never meant to end up at Happy Bellies. A little over a year ago, I left my mother's suburban home with my car packed full of everything I needed and nothing to make me remember what I was leaving behind. My belly was still soft from pregnancy, a room recently vacated. My plan had been to drive to White Sands. Hide in the dunes after the park closed, burrow like a sand snake, fall asleep pretending I was on the moon.

I had tried to be a mother, but I was a twenty-year-old kid, afraid of so many things. Afraid of the soft, pliant spot on the top of her head. Afraid of blog posts with titles like "What a good latch feels like." Afraid of how her chin looked like mine, and how that made me feel like I'd had something stolen from me.

I couldn't be a mother, but maybe I could be a snake in the sand.

My mother tried to stop me. She told me motherhood was supposed to be hard. She told me I was making a mistake and the only way to make amends for it was to grow up and do the responsible thing. I didn't tell her I'd already contacted an adoption agency. I didn't tell her it was already done.

I drove south with the windows down, like a teenager again. I saw signs for the Happy Bellies open house painted on plywood boards. They were the sorts of signs I normally wouldn't notice, signs that would blur as I drove past and blend into the desert. But now that I'd abandoned my old life, I felt I should accept every invitation, so I kept my eyes open and started paying attention to the new world I'd entered.

The sanctuary wasn't what it is now—only twenty-five pigs, only two pens—but I loved it anyway. Loved that most of the people who worked there seemed to be seasonal volunteers who came and went, impermanent and unattached. I loved the pigs, with their ugly, rubbery snouts and the flaky skin that turned out to be harder, rougher, than I'd imagined.

A woman named Pam led my tour group. She was sunburnt and sinewy. Her hair was completely silver, cropped short under her Celtics cap. She touched each pig on top of its head and greeted it by name as we approached.

I wondered aloud where so many pigs could have come from.

"Some of them are handed over, no questions asked," she told me, "by owners who flat-out quit. Some folks just decide they've had enough one day and give up caring, offload their burdens onto us." I liked her voice. I liked her New England drawl and her unashamed anger. "But most of them," she went on, "we rescue from abusive situations. Every month there are more pigs to save. Abused pigs making more abused pigs, on and on and on."

After the tour came to an end, I approached Pam as the others dispersed to their cars. I told her I wanted to work at Happy Bellies. I said I'd work for free in exchange for a place to stay.

"What sorts of things are you good at?" she asked.

"I don't sleep much," I said. "I'll work harder than anyone else." That wasn't an answer to her question. She shrugged, uninterested, started to turn aside. "Also," I added, trying to hold her attention, wanting to convince her I was worthwhile, something I wasn't even sure of myself, "I write things. I'm a sort of writer." It was partially true. I'd been an English major at NAU before I got pregnant and moved back home.

"Maybe I have something for you," Pam said.

She told me I could sleep on a cot in one of the offices if I could reliably put together the bi-weekly Happy Bellies newsletter. The newsletter went out to donors who liked to read little anecdotes about the pigs. I'd also have to write the occasional longer piece about what was happening at the sanctuary: new arrivals, repairs and renovations, things like that.

"Stories are good," said Pam. "Stories are what keep the donations coming."

I told her I could manage it.

"I'm shit at writing," she confessed. "I keep getting calls about misplaced commas."

Within two months I was also helping in the pens and Pam had put me on payroll.

Within six months I'd saved up enough to buy a trailer and move out of the office.

Sometimes, now, I wake early in the morning and look out my trailer window and see potbelly pigs playing in the last of the moonlight. The saguaros' shadows are long fingers reaching across their bristled backs. The pigs rear onto their hind legs and toss dried grass, confetti-like into the air. After a year of working at the sanctuary, I can name every pig on sight, even from this distance, even in the darkness. There's Othello and his sister, Pickles. There's Bigfoot, Esmerelda, Tiny Tim.

My trailer flanks the Active Seniors pen, though "active" is a relative term. People who sponsor the pigs like to bring toys in for their pigs to play with, and they're disappointed when they find that the pigs prefer to wallow in the kiddie pool or snuffle around the prickly pears before finding a shady space to nap. Our donors are mostly wealthy and eager-to-help retirees who live in the Foothills, people who remind me uncomfortably of my mother. The toys they bring in are always toys made for dogs, colorful ropes looped through rubber balls and cute, chew-resistant bunnies with squeakers hidden in their chests.

At night, when the donors and tour groups are gone, the toys fly. They get caught in the arms of the ocotillo. They arch over the fences into other pigs' pens. Like a spell has been cast over the sanctuary, the pigs become spry and limber. I've never been a good sleeper. Sometimes I lie awake all night, forgetting what sleep even feels like. But when I see the pigs play, I think that maybe I'm sleepless for a reason. Maybe I was born to bear witness to this pig joy.

My mind drifts to Thomas. Thinking about him now, I notice things I didn't when he was in front of me. I've always been this way. I notice more through memory than I do in the moment. I could live forever on a memory.

I focus hard on the memory of Thomas's hand gripping mine. He looks older than me, but he feels younger. He feels like someone who's never grieved.

I imagine kissing the corner of his drooping lips.

I imagine it as an experiment. I want to see what the fantasy of him can make me feel. I imagine him stepping toward me, but keeping the respectful space between us. He doesn't break eye contact. His body is stillness and control.

I leave my trailer before the sun rises. Bats flap silently overhead, shapes outlined against the stars. I break a sweat loading pig chow into a wheelbarrow. Midsummer days are too hot and the nights are too short for the temperature to drop below eighty-five.

By the time I make it to Lucy's pen, the sky is streaked with pink and doves are cooing in the saguaros. Lucy is still in her lean-to, spine facing out. A bucket of pig chow hangs from the crook of my elbow. I slap it with an open palm to let Lucy know I'm coming. We're keeping her in a private pen for the rest of the week while she recovers from her abortion.

Lucy's ears twitch, but she doesn't get up.

"Lucy," I say, "time for breakfast." Usually, the pigs are awake by sunrise and Lucy is the first to greet me at the gate every morning, a fast shape moving through the dark. Now, though, she doesn't move. I kneel in the dirt beside her, lay my head against her belly. I pretend I'm Sam Neill leaning into a sick triceratops, moving up and down with the rise and fall of her breathing. Pressing my ear hard against her skin, I listen for movements under the flesh. The gurgle, the whoosh of air in lungs, the heartbeat.

Lucy squirms under my weight, grunts, and stretches. She blows a puff of air from her nose, smacks her lips, and rolls onto her feet.

I sigh with relief and rise, stepping away from her to dump chow into her trough.

I watch her carefully as I shovel dung and use the hose to fill up her kiddie pool.

After Lucy finishes eating, she returns to her lean-to. She stands there, motionless, watching me. Like she's forgotten what it means to be herself.

I'm annoyed when I catch myself thinking, *She's missing her babies.*

"Hey," someone calls behind me. I turn to see Pam at the gate. "I need your help with a job today."

She tells me she's received a call about a hoarding case in South Tucson. A neighbor contacted the police about a backyard filled with pigs, and the police reached out to Happy Bellies after confirming the report.

"Up for it?"

I nod and scratch Lucy between the ears before going to my trailer to clean up. A little later, I meet Pam at her van. Her project over the past few months has been repurposing it into a pigmobile. Back seats removed, space partitioned into sections using a disassembled dog crate, the van now smells permanently of mud and manure and sweat.

Even after my year at the sanctuary, Pam remains a mystery to me. She doesn't talk about her life before Happy Bellies, which I appreciate, because it gives me permission to not talk about my own past, and I feel safe in this space of not-really-knowing each other. But today, as we fly down the highway, I have something I want to ask Pam.

"Do you think the pigs realize when they're pregnant?"

Pam repeats the question to herself, slowly, not taking her eyes off the road. "Do they realize?" she asks. "Do pigs *realize* they're pregnant?"

In her mouth, the question sounds silly. Something I learned about Pam early on is that she hates anthropomorphizing animals. She thinks it's insulting to them to assume their thoughts or feelings are anything like ours.

I'm about to tell her to forget it, never mind, when suddenly she says, "I dunno. I don't think it's so simple. I think what they feel is a pull." She squints into the bright desert morning, her silver hair whipped by the wind coming through the open window. "Kind of like how geese feel a pull south in the winter, and they don't question it. They just follow it. You always know when a pig's about to give birth 'cause it will start nesting in whatever it can find."

I wonder if Pam has a daughter or son she tries to forget about. I wonder, if I was going to make up a story for Pam, like I do for the pigs, what would I say?

We don't talk for the rest of the ride. The wind streams into the car in ribbons of heat that numb me quiet.

Pam drives us south, south, south. She pulls off the highway in an area of town I've seen once or twice before on similar missions. We drive over bumpy roads until she slows to a stop in front of an adobe house with a swing set in the front yard and a row of shriveled succulents in clay pots on the front porch. There are no cars in the driveway, but we get out anyway. The closest neighbor is a hundred feet away. The house is surrounded by gravelly desert, a few baby cacti poking out of the ground like headstones. The mailbox is so full that the door has dropped open and a mound of envelopes has grown on the ground.

The backyard is surrounded by a metal fence decorated with dried ocotillo branches. Pam tries the gate to the fence and swings it open easily. She takes a step through first. I follow.

I want to throw up at what I see.

There are fourteen pigs in the small dirt yard. A sprinkler leaks weakly, creating a puddle of shit. I step over a dead piglet in the mud. I can't stop myself from staring at its legs, unnaturally stiff, like they're balking at something. I gag and keep walking. A pig that looks like it must be part hog gnaws at the hose. All of the pigs are emaciated, thin enough that their ribs are showing. I've never seen a pig's ribs before.

Pam's jaw muscles tremble under her skin, but otherwise she is expressionless. "Back up the van to the gate," she says.

"Are we allowed to just take them?" I ask. "There's no one here. Aren't we supposed to get a license first?"

She looks at me, eyes ablaze. "Do you really care?"

Next to the van, I double over, hands hard against my knees. I heave into the dirt but nothing comes up. I spit. My saliva sizzles and evaporates in the heat.

It's clear no one has been home in weeks. How long had these pigs been left alone? My entire body is pulsing. I try to slow my breathing and feel sympathy for the person who left these pigs. Maybe they'd fallen on hard times. Maybe they'd gotten into an accident and were in hospital somewhere, paralyzed, wishing they could get back to their pets, unable to speak to let someone know that their beloved pigs were starving out here.

But no. Those pigs have never been loved.

I sit in the driver's seat while Pam uses a board to guide the pigs into the back. In case they're not tame. In case they bite. We're only able to fit three of the fourteen in the van, so Pam makes a call to Happy Bellies for a volunteer to drive down and pick up the rest.

As we pull back onto the highway, I turn and watch the pigs in the back. Three males. Their legs wobble as we change lanes. They don't try to break out of their partitions, as if they know the bars are there for their protection. But that's me anthropomorphizing again.

"Lucky pigs," I say to Pam. But we both know it's not true.

※

Pam tells me to take the rest of the day off. She'll find someone else to cover my last shift.

"Really?" It's uncharacteristic of Pam to give anyone a break, no matter what the circumstances. Once, one of the volunteers was pinned against a fence by a four-hundred-pound hog. She still had to do her evening rounds.

I wonder how traumatized I'd looked on the ride home.

I go back to my trailer. The air has been off all day, and I can feel the heat pressing against my skull like thumbs digging into my temples. I switch on the window unit. I fill my tiny kitchen sink with water and dunk my head under. Eyes closed, I hold my breath as long as I can. Water fills my ears and hair seaweeds around my neck.

I count to thirty, and when I can't hold my breath any longer, I lift my head.

The July newsletter is due at the printers by the end of the week and I still haven't written the main story. With my hair dripping down my back, I sit at my laptop and type: *Fourteen pigs were rescued from a backyard in South Tucson this week.*

Is "rescued" the right word? I don't like how it makes it sound like the pigs' struggle is over. What I really want to write about is the piglet dead in the mud. I dredge up the memory of it. Unlike their parents, baby potbelly pigs are all softness. Elf-like ears and round bellies. The piglet in the mud had a second skin of dried mud cracking along its back. It had flies swarming in its eyes.

I start to type, but then delete my words. One of the unspoken rules of the newsletter is that the stories need to be tragic but palatable. Not so tragic that anyone will want to turn away. Just tragic enough to entice people to help.

A thought intrudes: My daughter could be dead, and I'd never know. I'd go through life imagining her alive somewhere, going on family road trips to Yosemite, writing memoirs about what it means to be adopted, wearing flats to the prom instead of heels. None the wiser.

I close the laptop and lay on the floor of the trailer.

I bite down on my thumb until the thought goes away, or at least until its intensity fades.

I sit up just enough to grab the vet's business card from the counter, where I left it yesterday.

I type his number into my phone. He answers on the first ring, and I feel an unexpected twinge in my stomach.

"Hi," I say.

"Hello?"

"It's me. I mean, from Happy Bellies Sanctuary. We met the other day."

"I remember."

"Lucy's acting weird," I tell him.

I expect him to say, "Weird how?" He doesn't. Instead, he says, "I'll see you tomorrow."

We hang up.

I press my spine flat on the floor and focus on the firmness under my body.

※

In the morning, I go through my routine with one eye on the road. Every time dust swirls up in the distance, I think it's Thomas in his car. I realize we never discussed when he'd arrive.

Mid-morning, I check in with Lucy. She's eaten, which gives me hope. However, she doesn't leave her lean-to when I say her name.

By late afternoon, Thomas still hasn't arrived. I think about calling him, but I don't want to seem overly anxious.

I'm in the visitor center, using the table to make peanut butter sandwiches with medication hidden inside, when there's a knock on the door. Before I can answer, the door cracks open and Thomas pokes his head inside.

"Oh," I say, jumping to my feet and nearly knocking over a tower of sandwiches. I step forward and reach out to shake Thomas' hand but realize there's still peanut butter on my fingers. "Sorry," I say, pulling back.

Thomas stands in the doorway with his hands in his pockets, smiling pleasantly. He's dressed more casually today, in shorts and a T-shirt.

"I meant to be here earlier," he says, "but a couple of appointments ran late."

"It's fine," I say. "Should I bring Lucy into the clinic?"

He shakes his head. "How about you take me to her pen? Sometimes it's easier to see what's wrong with an animal if you see them on their home turf."

"Sure."

The pens are connected by a series of gates. Because we've added on pens as we've needed them, there's no easy way to travel between them. To get to one pen, you travel through another.

As we make our way to Lucy, I point out some of my favorite pigs. "There's Bubbles. He lived the first two years of his life in a bathtub. Now he loves running. He runs laps around his pen like he's a border collie. And Chuck. His owner only fed him strawberries. When we found him, his belly was so big his feet couldn't touch the ground."

"Where did you find Lucy?" he asks.

"Someone found her walking along the highway in Marana. We don't know where she came from."

I'm happy to see Lucy out of her lean-to, standing in the shade of a mesquite, when we reach her pen. "Hey, Luce," I say. She swings her tail from side to side.

Thomas approaches her slowly. He lets her sniff his hand before he squats and reaches out to feel beneath her belly. He closes his eyes as he presses three fingers into the soft space between her back legs and her teats.

I hover behind him while he works.

"What kinds of mothers are pigs?" I ask.

He glances back at me. "I'd expect you know better than I do."

"We've never had newborn piglets here. At least, not during my time."

Lucy snorts. Thomas pulls back his hand. Lucy digs her hooves into the dirt.

"Nothing seems unusual," Thomas says, rising to full height again and dusting off his palms with a clap. "It's normal for her to be experiencing cramps. I wouldn't worry if she is a little off for the next few days."

A hawk screams overhead. We both look up, shielding our eyes from the light. Still looking up, I take a step toward Lucy and rest a hand on top her snout. She growls, a deep throat sound. *You're okay,*

I'm about to say to her, *Everything will be okay*, but then I feel a sharp heat shoot through my forearm and I look down to find Lucy's mouth around my wrist. Teeth in my skin. Hair bristled in a Mohawk down her spine, tail swishing furiously from side to side. The sharp enamel of her incisors slips between my tendons, shears against the sides of my bones. The heel of my hand aches, threatens to shatter, under the pressure of her jaws.

Suddenly Lucy shifts her stance and loosens her grip. I didn't even realize I was struggling, but in the split-second that her grip weakens, I pull myself free.

My blood is on Lucy's chin. She bends her front legs, lowers her head. Thomas grabs me from behind and pulls me to the other side of the lean-to just as she charges at me. He holds my shoulder, guides me through the gate, and slams it shut behind us.

"What happened?" I ask. Lucy paces on the other side of the fence. I still feel her teeth in my wrist, trying to sever my veins. "What's wrong with her? Is she okay?"

Thomas pushes me forward, toward the visitor center. "We need to clean your wound. Now."

"No, no," I say, turning sharply in the other direction. "I don't want anyone to see this. My trailer. Let's go there."

I don't look at my hand as I lead the way. I can't stop seeing Lucy's body transformed into something I don't recognize. I've seen pigs turn before, but I've always spotted the warning signs. I march through the pens to my trailer with Thomas nearly clipping my heels. Did Lucy know it was me she was biting? She didn't try to bite Thomas when he touched her. Did she choose me for a reason? When an animal bites, it's not the animal's fault. I believe that. An animal is a reaction, its behavior the effect of a cause. Passing by the Active Seniors, I see the pigs raise their heads and snort. Can they smell the blood? Do they know what I've done? I think of the dead piglet in the mud, a piglet killed by people like me. The tusks of the Active Seniors are chrome in the blazing sun. Can the pigs read my mind? Are my thoughts leaking out for even animals to see?

The door to my trailer is unlocked, as always. I shoulder it open, hustle inside, collapse onto my narrow couch. "First-aid kit is in the kitchenette," I say to Thomas. "Top drawer on the left."

Thomas grabs it swiftly and kneels on the floor and daubs alcohol onto my wrist.

I feel a pressure behind my eyes and I wonder if I'm about to cry.

Thomas takes a breath. He says, "The average gestation period for a potbelly pig is three months, three weeks, and three days."

I'm trying to get better at forgetting things. I want to make myself forget my daughter's birthday. I'm close. I forget the date but I still remember that it was sometime late in the summer. I remember a monsoon had flooded the streets. I was at my then-boyfriend's apartment when my water broke. I try to forget that my wrist is on fire, try to forget why.

"Mother pigs are grumpy and clumsy. A mother pig will sometimes accidentally crush her piglets during labor." Thomas wraps a strip of gauze around my wrist and pulls it tight.

I think of the geese feeling a pull south and not questioning it, just answering. I try to breathe my brain quiet. When I left my daughter, was it because I'd felt a pull to? Or was it because it felt logical? I had made list after list of reasons her life and my life would be better off disentangled.

"You're going to need stitches," Thomas tells me. He helps me stand, and I hold tight to his arm.

I imagine a pig walking down the highway, hooves clacking on cracked pavement. A pig walking through the boundless desert, stomping through forests of cholla that reach out for flesh to scar. A pig looking for her piglets, snuffling through the dirt, sniffing at the hazy air, trying to catch their scent, trying to see some trace of them. The sky. The sand. The empty horizon. They could be anywhere.

Forever Baby

after Stardew Valley

ONE DAY YOUR DAUGHTER STOPS GROWING UP. You notice right away. Her fingernails are the same exact length that they were yesterday. You count her eyelashes, you count the freckles on her cheeks, you count her teeth. All the same. She is two years old.

When you were pregnant, other mothers would tell you that the baby stage is the best. You and your child, raw together in a bright, new world. They told you to savor those moments, that you'd miss them once they'd passed. But even after she was born, you couldn't wait for your baby to grow up. You ached for the day when she'd be old enough to speak. Old enough for you to teach her things. Like how to catch a Woodskip in the secret woods, how to pan gold from the lakes, or how to make friends with Krobus in the tunnels beneath the cemetery.

You'd spent your life tilling fields, fending off the encroaching weeds and fallen logs, looking for ways to grow your tomatoes fatter, your grape vines vinier. You'd raised buildings. Incubated eggs in beds of hay. You'd taken your sword and pickaxe into the caves, found the end of every secret passageway. All you knew was a life of ambition and forward movement.

On the day your daughter stops growing up, she spends an hour staring at a beam of light traveling across the floor. You watch her from the kitchen and try to make a mental list of every word she knows. The average two-year-old can speak about seventy words. Does your daughter know more than that? Less? Are there words you don't know to count? Maybe ones she's spoken only to herself, alone at night in her bed.

You decide not to worry yet. Maybe this is just a phase she is going through. Maybe all children stop growing up at some point, and then start up again. Like a plant hibernating in the cold.

Summer moves forward. Your daughter dashes through the house like a bird caught in a gale. Every morning you count her freckles, measure the length of her hair. One night, after her bath, you trim one of your daughter's thumb nails with a pair of scissors. You want to prove that your daughter is still capable of change, or capable of being changed. You trim the nail so short that you accidentally nick the skin. As your daughter wails, you dab at the blood with a tissue. You kiss the top of her head and apologize until she's lulled to sleep and you can tip-toe to your own bed. The next morning, the first thing you do is go to your daughter to check the cut. But it has healed. Or, more accurately, it has completely disappeared. The trimmed nail is exactly the same length as it had been the morning before. You touch the spot on her skin where you'd made her bleed. She doesn't flinch at all.

Autumn comes. Your daughter falls asleep in her tiny, four-post bed, like a sea maiden floating out to sea. Spiders flee indoors to build cobwebs in corners. Leaves change colors from the inside out. Your house fills with pumpkins big and small, and your daughter likes to stack the smallest into tall, teetering towers. All day, she wanders around the house in nothing but a diaper, completely unashamed, unaware of the difference between being naked and being clothed.

Later, raking leaves around the chicken coop, you think of a time when you were fifteen and drunk for the first time at a party. Your ride had left without you, and you had to call your mother to pick you up. Sitting in the front seat of her car, you felt exposed and embarrassed in your tank top, your mother's eyes on the lacy bra visible through the fabric. You'd bought it with your own money at the mall last Saturday, had been hiding it under your bed, afraid of what your mother would assume if she found it while putting away the wash.

Halfway home, you puked into the backseat. *Ugh, I'm sorry, Mom*, you said. *I'll clean it up. I'm sorry. I'm sorry.* The worst part was your mother's silence. She didn't speak until you were home and she was tucking you into bed. She hadn't tucked you in for years. Your vision spun, and all you could do was look up at her as she placed your arms under the covers and propped your head up with pillows. As she turned off the lights, she paused in the doorway and sighed. "I wish I still had my baby," she said, and closed the door behind her.

You understood in that moment that you were no longer the daughter your mother wanted. In fact, you had replaced her. Your mother had wanted a child, but she didn't want this adult you were becoming. Every day you grew farther away from the fantasy she'd had of you. This thought made you sad for yourself but also sad for your mother.

When you learned you were pregnant, you swore to never mourn the versions of herself your daughter left behind. You wouldn't mourn the sound of her laughing alone in her crib in the early morning. You wouldn't mourn her letters to Santa Claus, signed in awkward cursive. When your daughter got her first tattoo, you wouldn't mourn the skin she covered up. You wouldn't just love these new versions of your daughter; you'd welcome and like them.

But now you find yourself mourning all these future versions of your daughter you will never meet. Your mother had wished for a for-ever-baby, and now her wish is your curse.

Fall becomes winter. Every day for the past six months, your child has woken up as the same child. On the morning of the first snow, you bring handfuls of white snow into the house and your daughter eats it. Stuffs her mouth full, then cries when it melts and dribbles down her chin.

You read in a child development book that children don't start growing kneecaps until age three. That toddlers are ambidextrous. That two-year olds don't understand yet that their mind is separate from other people's.

You understand now that this is how it will always be. This isn't a phase. You will grow old, and your baby will continue to be your baby. Continue to stack pumpkins like blocks, continue to take handfuls of snow in her fists and expect it to stay snow forever. Just as you can count on Krobus to always be in the sewers, and the dwarf to always be in the caves, and the wizard to always be in his tower. You hope those other mothers were right. You hope the baby stage will be the best.

You wipe away the melted snow dripping down your daughter's neck with the end of your sleeve. Then you take her hand. You notice that her fist fits perfectly inside your own, like a nut inside a shell.

"Want to see more snow?" you ask your daughter.

"Snow," she says. Neither of you are wearing shoes or jackets, but you lead her outside onto the front porch anyway. The warmth of the house still sticks to your skin and your clothes, and it will be a minute before you feel the cold. Your daughter reaches out, waiting for the snow to find her open palm, and you do the same.

The Earth Room

THERE'S AN APARTMENT in the city that's filled, wall to wall, with three feet of level earth. The first time J. takes me home with him, he teaches me to crawl through the space: slow and patient, fingers outstretched. "So that you don't sink through," he explains. "Pretend you're crossing ice."

In what must have once been a bedroom, we lie on our backs with only the edges of our hands touching. There are no paintings on the walls. No photographs or mirrors. No doors. There's no furniture, not even a bed. Only earth. It's very soft and very, very quiet. The smell reminds me of freshly dug holes, of upturned stones, of dripping caves. It reminds me of childhood summers spent wrestling through the woods behind my house. Peering into groundhog holes, looking for salamanders under rotting leaves. The smell overwhelms me with a nostalgia I hadn't realized I harbored.

"How long has this been here?" I ask J.

He tells me it was just a habit at first. On walks in the park, he'd fill his pockets with handfuls of peat moss or dirt from planters and shake them empty when he arrived home. He liked getting out of bed and feeling dirt under his bare feet. He liked the way it absorbed the roar of the city. He wanted more. He started ordering bags of planting soil. Hundreds of pounds of it, hundreds of dollars, delivered to his apartment weekly. When neighbors questioned him, he told them he was cultivating an indoor garden. Heirloom tomato plants. Butterfly palms to clear toxins from the air.

"One time," he said, "I forgot to pay my bills for a month and didn't even notice when my electricity was shut off. I rarely cooked at home anyway, and I stopped turning on the lights long ago." All day, he said, the sun casts a moving square of light through his curtainless windows onto the dirt. At night, the streetlights brighten the rooms.

I curl my hands into claws and dig in my fingers, almost up to my wrists. I imagine how later I'll have to pick the dirt out from under my nails, how I'll carry a bit of this place across the city with me. I ask, "How much *is* there?"

J. thinks for a moment. "I did the math once. It's somewhere north of a hundred tons. You know what else weighs that much? A radio tower. A space shuttle. A railroad locomotive engine."

He props himself up on his elbow, leans over to kiss me. As we kiss, I feel myself sinking into the soil a little. The kiss deepens. The earth pulls me closer.

When the kiss ends, we both laugh and look away a little shyly. It's been a long time since a man has been shy with me. I like it.

"I guess I should go," I say. I pause to see if he'll stop me, but he doesn't. I sit up and brush myself off. When I glance back over my shoulder, I notice the impression I made in the earth. It disturbs me a little to see this echo of my body. I smooth it over with my hands.

"Goodnight," I say.

In the darkness, he's quiet.

I moved to the city a year ago with a boyfriend I thought I'd marry. I found a job. I found a sushi place that was better than any I'd had in the last town. I ate there often enough for the hostess to automatically bring me a cup of hot sake when I sat down, but not so often that she knew me by name. And then the boyfriend I thought I'd marry didn't even want to be my boyfriend anymore. I had to find a new apartment to live in, in a new part of the city. A new sushi restaurant. A new route to work, along unfamiliar sidewalks lined with unfamiliar vendors.

During this time, I felt a hollow open inside me. That hollow was home to something dark and squirming, something that was both me and not me. I did everything I could to ignore it. When I wasn't working, I'd take the subway to the park and power walk the trails until my lungs burned. Or I'd sit on a bench and watch the street performers. My favorite was a man who'd use a hula hoop to make gigantic bubbles that would drift over the sidewalk like blind whales before they got caught in the branches of trees and bursting. It was here, at the park, that I met the man with the apartment full of earth. After a few weeks of haunting the trails and benches I started noticing him. He also seemed to spend a lot of time on a bench doing nothing at all. Another week passed, and he started to notice me, too. We began to sit on the same bench.

He told me he went by J., like an abbreviation. He was one of those men who looked both young and old at the same time. I could tell he was older than me, though I wasn't sure if it was only by a couple of years or over a decade. He often wore gray corduroys and a black peacoat. He had nice hands with delicate knuckles. I asked him to walk with me. As we strolled through the park, our shoulders raised against the cold, I felt the hollow inside myself shrink. I started to feel again like a version of myself I recognized.

The day after I visit J.'s apartment, I wander through the city feeling dizzy. My head has become a bowl full of dirt. I go to work. I drink coffee. I type emails in a cubicle overexposed to light. I squint into my computer screen.

In the bathroom, I roll my sleeves up to my elbows. I turn the water on hot and wait until it's steaming before I plunge in my arms. As I wash, dirt forms trails on my skin and puddles in the sink before it disappears down the drain. I try to imagine what J.'s apartment must have looked like with just an inch of earth, or a foot, or two. It's like a game

I used to play as a child, when I'd drape myself upside down from the couch and try to convince myself that the ceiling was the floor, that the house as I knew it wasn't what it seemed. I imagine J.'s furniture slowly becoming submerged in earth, the rugs disappearing, then framed photographs of family, then the couch, the kitchen table. I wonder if he removed the furniture long ago, or if it was still there.

I realize I've been standing with my arms in the water for too long. My skin has blanched and wrinkled. I return to my desk to find one of my co-workers waiting for me. She asks me about a project we're working on together, asks for numbers I should remember but don't. I can't seem to focus on her face. She stops in the middle of a sentence. She tells me I should go home early. I don't look so good.

"Yeah," I say, "Maybe you're right."

It's barely ten in the morning. Outside the building I smell shawarma and car exhaust. I could retreat to familiar surroundings, take the subway south, bunker down in my loft above the Jamaican restaurant where, from morning to night, I can hear the chefs shouting over the sound of clinking dishes. My apartment always smells like festivals and fried plantains and the meat special of the day. I loved those smells when I first moved in, though lately they've left me disoriented. I feel like a dog in a park, losing itself in a plethora of scents. So, I think of J.'s apartment. The cool earth under my palms. The simplicity of a space filled with nothing but earth. I walk north. If I change my mind, I tell myself, I can always hop on a subway or call a cab to take me home.

When J. had taken me home, last night, I'd been surprised to realize he lived in my old neighborhood, just a couple blocks from where I'd lived with my ex. I'd walked by his building a hundred times, never knowing that a mass of earth of impossible weight was suspended above me. It makes me wonder what other apartments contain. As I walk now, I imagine an apartment full of sea water, full of hornets, full of fur. I start to see the city as a world full of hidden pockets, of self-contained worlds existing inside the larger world.

I arrive at J.'s building and slip inside as someone else is leaving. I climb the stairs to the third story. A moment of doubt stops me in the hallway; I'm unsure which door belongs to him. But then I remember the windows letting in streetlight and I walk to the end of the hall:

310. I knock. No-one answers. No sound of footsteps from the other side of the door, though I remind myself there wouldn't be. I knock again. I wait.

I'm tired, so tired, and under my clothes I feel sweaty. Maybe I walked too fast, too long in the heat, or maybe I'm feverish. The thought of descending the stairs and staggering home makes me want to cry.

When I put my hand on the cool knob and turn it, the door swings outward with ease.

A three-foot wall of earth stands in front of me.

I crawl up onto the earth and pull the door closed behind me.

"Hello?" I say into the cool darkness of the apartment. But I already know the place is empty. Without doors, you can see inside every room from the entryway.

I crawl to the bedroom as J. taught me to do: slow and patient, fingers outstretched. The earth has a texture like wet moss under my palms. In the bedroom, I drop onto my side and the earth embraces me. I can already feel it cooling my body, bringing me back to normal. I sigh and close my eyes.

When I open my eyes again, I find a small mushroom growing from the ground just a few inches in front of my face. It has a white dome and a pinkish stalk. I reach out and pluck it from the soil. It resists slightly, but dislodges with mycelium trailing from its end. It is light and feathery. I wonder how it'd taste, and as I wonder this, I'm already placing it on my tongue. It's earthy. A little spicy. I know I should spit it out, but I feel somehow as if this moment has already been written and I already know that I will swallow the mushroom. I do. I swallow it whole. I don't even feel it moving down my throat.

I imagine the mushroom rooting itself in my belly, its mycelium traveling through my bloodstream, tendrils reaching out through all the hollow parts of me.

The earth is cool against my hot skin.

The mushroom in my belly releases spores that grow new mushrooms. Caps umbrella-open in my throat, between my pelvic bones.

Outside, a tree taps its branches against the window.

My body is part fungi.

I let my eyelids drop.

When I wake up, I find J. sitting cross-legged in the earth beside me. He holds a hand to my forehead.

I sit up, my tongue dry. I wipe at my mouth with the backs of my fingers, and when I pull away there's dirt on my lips. I have no idea how long I've slept. The apartment is mostly dark now, and I can see the orange glow of the streetlights coming through the windows. I'm still in my work clothes: chunky heels, slacks, a buttoned-up cardigan.

"I was sick today," I say. "I left the office early. I'm sorry, I shouldn't have come here, I don't know why I did. The door was open."

In J.'s lap are two large Styrofoam containers with lids. "Ramen," he says. "I went out for dinner while you were still asleep. How are you feeling now?"

"Better," I say. It's true. My fever has broken. I feel so much better that part of me wonders if my sickness had been only in my head. "There was a mushroom," I say. "Before I fell asleep."

"Sometimes that happens," says J. "I always think of this as a place that never changes, but then I'll be surprised by something that crawls out of the ground."

I want to ask him if he knows what kind of mushroom it was, but then he might ask to see it and I'd have to admit I ate a mushroom I couldn't identify — ate it just because I could.

J. begins to peel the lids off the ramen. For a second, with his head dipped into the steam rising from the broth, he looks like someone else, like someone I might have dated once. For a second, my pulse quickens and I feel that hollowness under my ribcage, that familiar dark, that squirmy space, reminding me it hasn't gone away. I imagine the mycelium in my stomach twitching towards the hollowness, stretching to fill it. But the feeling passes. Now I have a warm container of ramen in my lap, and J. is smiling at me, and things are okay again.

❧

My last boyfriend, the boyfriend I thought I'd marry, took up a new hobby every six months or so. First, it was Dungeons and Dragons campaigns, hosted in our living room every Sunday. Then it was glass-blowing. Then woodcarving. He liked me to be involved in his hobbies with him, so I was. I fought hobgoblins with my level-2 druid spells. I blew green glass goblets to go along his blue ones. I sanded down the barely-recognizable animal figures he'd carved with his Swiss Army knife.

When we moved to the city, he signed us up for pottery classes. Everything I made came out of the kiln feeling impossibly heavy. Bowls made for Vikings. Mugs made for giants. He used the bowls and mugs anyway, despite their impracticality. The first time I saw him sipping coffee from something I'd made, I thought he was trying to be funny. But he wasn't. He really liked my mugs. I added that to the list of reasons we should be together. I had a running list I kept without really trying to. Anyway, pottery was probably his favorite of all the hobbies he ever picked up. He was still doing it when we broke up, filling our then-shared apartment with vases and bowls and plates the size of frisbees. He said he liked that we were making art out of a raw material that had taken thousands of years to form. Some clay deposits had been hidden underground for millennia before someone stumbled upon them. "Nothing can hide underground forever," he told me.

๛

After dinner, J. asks me to spend the night.

I start to shake my head, and he says, "No pressure. But you're sick. You should rest."

I think about refusing, but he's right. Though my fever has broken, my apartment feels as if it's a whole country away. Just imagining the miles of underground subway tunnels separating me from my bed makes me tired.

I lie on my side, facing J. He lies next to me, looking up at the ceiling, a respectful space between us. In the other room, the walls change from green to yellow to red.

"I remember the sickest I've ever been," J. says suddenly. "I was seven or eight. It was nighttime, and I was alone in my bedroom. All I could see was a sliver of light under my door. My parents were in the living room, watching television, but I couldn't call to them, no matter how hard I tried. I kept hallucinating that one of them would come to my door and I'd ask for water, but then they'd leave, and the hallucination would start all over again."

This is the first time he's told me anything about his past. I want to ask where he grew up. Where his parents were now. How many people, other than me, know about this space full of earth. But before I can do that, he's asleep, snoring lightly. The sound is soft and pleasant, like wind moving through a tunnel. I watch him in the artificial light, looking for that shape-shifting quality I'd seen in his face earlier, but this time he just looks like himself.

As I wait for sleep to descend on me, I can't help thinking of what he said earlier — about things that grow up out of his floor and surprise him. A handful of soil can contain between one hundred and one thousand arthropods, smaller than the eye can see, and up to fifty billion bacteria. I imagine all the invisible worlds teeming under our feet, transforming and evolving as we eat, as we sleep, as we brush skin. Every now and then something grows big enough to break the surface.

I want to find something. I want to find something that isn't supposed to be here. A fairy's circle. A subterranean stream bubbling to the surface. A hibernating box turtle the size of a dinner tray.

I roll onto my hands and knees and crawl into the living area. I go to the windows, thinking that this is where things are most likely to grow, fed by sunlight and the artificial colors of the city. I bring my face close to the earth. It's musky, sweet, and smooth.

I start to dig. I dig with my fingers, push dirt out of the way with my arms, my elbows. I wonder if I could keep digging to reach the first dirt. Dirt he dropped here years ago, during a different time in his life.

I'm nearly a foot down when my fingers scrape against something hard. I reach in deeper and close my fist around it and pull it loose from the ground. I open my hand to find a twenty-sided die, still caked in dirt, resting in my palm. I stare at it. It's emerald, with white numbers. The edges are dulled and rounded down. It's been well-used.

I shake my head.

I drop the die back into the hole, but I don't bury it. I leave the hole as it is. I crawl back into the bedroom and lay down in the hollow my body made before I left.

J. talks in his sleep. "Who was he?" he mumbles. "He's here." He gasps.

I pick the dirt out from under my fingernails. I wait for J.'s breathing to return to normal.

I leave at dawn, so I have enough time to return to my own apartment and change before heading into work.

All morning at my desk, I think of the hole I dug in the apartment, the hole containing the die. I have this feeling that if I'd kept digging, I would have found more. I both want to and don't want to see what else the earth contains. I try to throw myself into my work, but I can't focus on what I'm supposed to be doing. My arms feel electric, as though the mushroom's mycelium have wormed into my muscles and are fighting to take control of me. I close my eyes and rest my face in my palms. In my mind, I'm tunneling through J.'s apartment. My cells have been digested by the mushroom and transformed into earth. My body belongs to the ground. I decide I'll go back. I tell myself I'm just confused about what I found. All I need to do is see the apartment in the light of day, to know everything is okay. As soon as I've made this decision, I feel better.

I leave the office at noon. When I reach his apartment, the door is unlocked, just like yesterday. And just like yesterday, J. is gone. I return to the hole I'd dug in the night. It's undisturbed. I reach in and find the twenty-sided die. It's warm, as if it has spent the day clutched in someone's sweaty palm. I place it on the earth next to me, then I take off my work jacket so it doesn't get dirty, I roll up the hem of my dress past my knees, and I kneel in the dirt by the hole and dig down further than before.

It's such a relief to be digging. I love the feeling of loose earth in my hands. I love the changes in the smell and the color, the deeper I dig. Before long, I've found something else. I blow off the dirt. A Swiss Army knife. I place it next to the die. I keep digging. Next, I find a blue glass goblet. I wipe the dirt off the rim with my thumb. My hands are shaking.

Did J. leave these items here for me? Or did they leave themselves?

I feel like I'm getting close to the bottom. Part of me wants to run away, but another part of me must keep going. What will happen when I reach the floor?

Before I can find out, I hear the door close behind me.

I turn. J. is on his knees, watching me.

Except it's not J. Or it is J., but he's also someone else. It's like when you're walking through an airport, and you think you recognize someone you know, someone close to you, like your brother, and you're sure it's him, but then you see the stranger from a different angle and it's clearly not him, and you have no idea how you confused him for someone else in the first place.

The man in front of me is J.

The man is also my ex.

He has my ex's dark eyebrows and deep-set eyes. But he has J.'s thin face, J.'s long eyelashes. And as I look more closely, I realize he doesn't just look like my ex; he looks like every boy I've ever loved.

"Who am I?" he says.

I wait for that hollow to widen inside me. To fill me with terror. I expect it to get so wide I'll feel it taut under my skin. But I don't. I feel solid. I feel heavy.

I reach out and take his hand.

"It's okay," I say.

We lower ourselves into the hole I've dug. Together, inside, we continue to dig. We find more things. A class ring I wore only once. A state champion tennis medal. A beaded bracelet I recognize from my tenth birthday. A chipped water glass. Other objects, objects I don't recognize, objects from someone else's life. We dig. After a while, the earth starts to collapse back in on us, burying our legs, our waists, our chests. And we don't push it away. We let ourselves join the snaking strands of mycelium, the earthworms, the small creatures that have not yet woken up.

I Change You

THE FIRST TIME MY GIRLFRIEND turned me into an animal, we'd only been dating for two months. I woke in the middle of the night to her side of the bed cold, the covers pushed back. Still half asleep, I wandered through her dark apartment, feeling for the door frame, for the knob. I'd forgotten to put on my glasses, and when I opened the bathroom door, the room swirled with white mist. My girlfriend sat in the clawfoot tub, water to her waist. Her edges blurred. Her skin fractured light.

"Tam," I said, and she gasped. Her arms curled around herself. And in that same moment, I became a salamander.

I didn't know I was a salamander at first. I just knew that I had become small. I could smell the water in the air, could hear the pop of soap bubbles in the bath like tiny bells.

Tam stepped out of the tub, reaching for a towel. She dripped puddles onto the tile, and I felt myself drawn to them. My skin shivered with the feeling.

"I'm so sorry," she said, gently nudging me into her palm. "I'm so sorry. It was an accident. I swear I didn't mean to."

My toes clung to her skin. I could feel the pores in her finger pads. I flicked my tongue, and could taste the sweetness of her sweat. I'd never felt closer to her, never loved her more, never felt loved by her more. She took me to bed, kept me safe in the curled basket of her fingers. By morning, I was a man again.

"This happened with my high school boyfriend," she said, sitting cross-legged in the bed next to me. "I'd get annoyed by something small, and suddenly he'd be a moth. Or a hedgehog. Or a little turtle." She pulled the blankets up over her lap. She spoke in a disjointed way when she was nervous, putting long spaces between her words, like she couldn't catch her breath. "I dated a few guys in college, but it never happened again. The animal thing. I thought it was something I'd grown out of. The way kids grow out of wetting the bed or getting warts."

I wrapped an arm around Tam's shoulders, let her lean her face into my neck. Now that I'd tasted her sweat, now that I'd felt my feet suction-cupped to her skin and spent a night sleeping in her palm, I noticed things about her that I didn't before. The three strands of silver hair that grew behind her ear. The fact that her blinks were exactly ten seconds apart. The cluster of blue veins on her inner ankle.

"I know this is a lot," said Tam, pulling away.

"It's okay," I replied mechanically, but it was the truth. I'd known when we started dating that Tam had a bit of magic to her, I just didn't know how much. "We can make this work."

❧

The second time Tam turned me into an animal, I became a bat. We'd been watching her favorite childhood movie. She'd been so excited to share it with me, but I was distracted that night, never laughed at the right moments, spent too much time looking at my phone.

"Fine," she'd snapped eventually, turning off the movie. "We don't have to watch it." And suddenly, I was flapping circles around the ceiling fan. The room around me lost its definition. Time slowed down. I could count every rotation of the fan blades.

The third time, she turned me into a snail. She'd been speeding in a parking lot. I'd told her, maybe more harshly than I needed to, to slow down. As a snail, I glided across the car seat, leaving a silvery trail on the fabric. The world was colorless, full of large shadows and explosions of light. I felt her pick me up, place me on the bare round of her shoulder. My brain sparked with the texture of the fine hairs on her skin. Her lips moved, and I couldn't hear a sound, but my body tingled with the vibration of her words.

I lost track of the reasons Tam changed me.

She made me a baby caiman. An elf owl. A bullfrog.

She made me a gila monster. She made me a lightning bug.

Tam was always sorry afterwards. She'd take me into her arms and stroke my fur or my scales or my exoskeleton and whisper apologies into my skin. "I didn't mean it," she always said. But after a few months, I started to wonder if she had more control over her power than she claimed.

Once, Tam turned me into a goat for an entire day. By the time I transformed back, it was dusk, I had a mouthful of grass, and the over-grown weeds in her backyard had been gnawed to their roots. Another time, she turned me into a spider. When I was a man again, my belly was heavy with mosquitos and flies, and Tam was dusting webs from the corners. I began to wonder if she changed me out of convenience rather than out of anger.

But it was difficult for me to ever hold onto these worries for long. As an animal, I'd rest my body against the warm swell of her stomach, her breaths soothing me to sleep, and I'd forgive her of everything. Every animal I became would give me a new reason to love her. The short, dark hairs on the back of her neck. The smell behind her knees, a smell that reminded me of the wind that blows out of the forest at night. The tiny blood vessels shaped like splintered lightning in her eyes. Details I wouldn't have noticed as a human.

I never thought of the possibility that she'd break up with me.

We were eight months into our relationship. She invited me out to a bar I'd never been to before. It was the kind of place that has only eight cocktails on the menu, each varnished with a bundle of fresh herbs tied with lemon rind.

"This place used to be a funeral home," Tam told me as we found a seat on a pew in the back corner of the space. The only light came from antique, stained glass lamps and tealight candles on the tables. "They used to embalm bodies in the basement."

We sipped our drinks and traced shapes in the condensation on our glasses.

Tam took a breath. "I think we need to take some time apart." She saw my expression and said gently, "Don't act surprised. You must have known this was coming. For months now it's been the same. We get on each other's nerves. I change you."

I don't mind, I wanted to say.

She placed a hand on my knee and held my eyes. "Every relationship ends somewhere. Why shouldn't ours end here?"

༜

So, I stopped seeing Tam.

On weekends, when in the past I'd spend all my time with her, I now drove to the woods. I didn't follow a trail. Instead, I'd find a crow to follow. Or a creek. Or a toad hopping through the mud.

Those senses I gained when I became an animal, they never truly left me.

I'd see a mushroom growing on a trunk and ache to scrape its flesh with my teeth. I'd feel a weight to the air and know it would rain soon. But, in my human body, reading the world around me was like trying to see through static.

At night, I could no longer get comfortable in my body. My hips were too solid, jutting out of me like stone. My feet were heavy and loud. I dreamed of having a skeleton small enough to fit in Tam's pocket. Of being a vampire bat, able to smell the heat of her blood from the air.

A month after we split up, I walked to Tam's building. It was late, but I texted her until she buzzed me in. I sprinted up the three flights of stairs to her apartment. I found her in her doorway, hand on hip.

It was incredible how little she'd changed. She still wore the extralarge, white T-shirt that she'd slept in every night with me. A single black hair tie on her wrist. A mole on each cheek. Flecks of mascara under her eyes.

"I don't think you should come in," she said.

I crouched, hands on my knees, catching my breath. My whole body hurt with its humanness.

"Change me," I gasped. "One more time."

She laughed. "You don't want that. Go home. You'll feel better in the morning." She turned back to her apartment, started to pull the door closed.

"Wait," I said, and she did. I stood up straighter, stepped closer. "Listen. The best, simplest times were when we were together like that. Maybe there's a reason you could change me. Maybe it was meant to be that way."

Tam let out a frustrated sigh. She curled her hand into a fist and pressed it into her forehead. I wished I was a fox that could wrap around her ankles. I wished I was a canary that could build a nest in her hair. I wanted to touch her in a way she'd welcome. I wanted touch that was just touch.

"Listen," Tam said. I could feel her trying to make her breaths slow, her voice steady. "I used to think all girls could turn boys to animals. I thought of it like an old, inherited magic passed from mother to daughter. But I was wrong. You can't imagine how lonely it is to be who I am."

"Please," I tried again. "Change me and I'll stay forever. You won't have to be lonely."

I could feel her fighting it. But the angrier she was with me, the more I felt my skin shiver.

"Please," I said. I took a step towards her.

I took another step.

And with the next step, I changed.

My hooves clacked on the tiles. My antlers knocked against the ceiling. I felt the urge to jump, to leap. I felt I could jump as high as I wanted, clear any hedge, any brook. I was a buck in the king's wood, pursued by baying hounds. I was a buck on the tundra, wolves' breath hot against my flank.

Still in her doorway, Tam covered her face with her hands. I didn't understand why she was so sad. I placed my soft lower lip on her wrist. I nibbled her like she was the sweetest apple. I nudged her hands with my nose, then with my cheek. Now, when I smelled her, she would also smell a little bit like me. And that's how I'd know I belonged to her.

Chew

I can't tell if my dog loves or hates the bones.

She finds them wherever we go. A bone in the parking lot. A bone under the mesquite tree. She finds bones where bones don't belong. A bone in my backpack. A bone under the passenger's seat of my car. A bone under the covers of my bed. When my dog finds a bone, she carries it home. She plops down on the couch with a sigh, holds it between her paws. Gnaws until her mouth foams. Gnaws until her gums bleed.

Every bone is a little different. Some are long and bowed. Others are tiny, shaped like the spine of a feather. Once, she finds a bone that looks so much like a human clavicle that I worry one day she'll realize I am a body containing a skeleton. On the internet, I learn that humans are born with two hundred and seventy bones, but as we grow, some of them fuse together, and by the time we're adults, we have only two hundred and six. That's still a lot. I have nightmares in which I wake to my dog's teeth locked around my wrist. *You have so many,* she says in my dreams. *Just give me one.*

When I wake, I try to hide the gnawed-up bones somewhere she won't find them, but she always finds them. She finds the bone I hide in the crisper drawer of the refrigerator, the one I hide it in the bathtub behind the shower curtain, even the one I bury in the backyard under a creosote bush to throw her off the scent.

Sometimes I can distract her from the bones. I distract her with jogs around the neighborhood, with trips to the pet store for chew toys shaped like ferrets, with long hikes in the mountains south of our home. But I see her eyes drifting from what's in front of us. She's always searching for the next bone, and as long as she's searching for it, she finds it.

One night, tired of fighting, I let her take a rabbit's rib into bed. I let her sleep at my feet with it tucked beneath her paws. When I wake in the morning, the bone looks different. Still tucked under my dog's whiskery chin, it's now nearly the length and thickness of my arm. One end has sprouted what looks like little antler nubs. I leap out of bed, like the bone might grow hands and reach for me through the sheets. I pick up an old shirt from the floor and use it as a glove to carefully pull the bone out from under my dog without waking her. Then, in my sleep shirt and bare feet, I dash into the side yard and throw it in the green garbage bin, slam it shut.

In the bathroom, I wash my hands with soap and water, get dressed, and brush my teeth. I try to breathe in through my nose, out through my mouth. Through the window, I can see the trash bin. It's still four days until trash pickup. I imagine the bone cradled between bags of warm garbage, growing legs through the afternoon, growing talons, growing fangs.

I put on my tennis shoes. I go back outside with a black trash bag and open the bin. The bone hasn't changed in the thirty minutes since I threw it away. I take that as a good sign. I hold my breath, reach in, knot the bone inside the empty bag. Then I leash my dog.

Together we walk down the street and into the dry river wash. We walk past the chollas, past the family of quails' *chip-chirp*ing into the underbrush, past veins carved into the sand by flash floods last July. I carry the bone in the bag, arm outstretched so it doesn't swing against my leg.

After we've been walking for twenty minutes, I loop my dog's leash around my wrist, drop onto my hands and knees, and dig. I dig with my hands, with my nails. It isn't easy, because as soon as I make any progress, the hole collapses in on itself, the dry sand and dirt and bits of rock unable to hold a shape. I don't realize until I stop to wipe sweaty strands of hair from my eyes with the back of my hand, that while I've been digging, my dog has torn through the bag and is holding the bone in her jaws, tail wagging, looking at me expectantly.

No, I say. *Drop it. Drop it.*

I don't want to touch it, but I do. I grab the bone by its knubby antlers, pull and pull until it slips out of my hands. I hook my fingers between my dog's jaws and try to pry them open like I crack open the shell of a pistachio. Her tail wagging the whole time, like she knows my fingers are no match for her mouth built for tearing sinew from skeleton, capable of felling a grown antelope. I give up and sit cross-legged next to her in the dirt. She sits, too, bone between her paws. I can see the muscles in her head moving as she chews, muscles I didn't even know she had. Her eyes bulge.

She looks straight at me as she chews. I wonder if maybe the bone didn't grow on its own, but grew through some magic stored in her. Old, dog magic passed down from wolves, magic no human has been able to domesticate away. I wish I could speak in a language she'd understand. If I could, I'd ask her about the magic. I'd ask her why she chews. I'd ask her what ancient call she's trying to answer by gnawing at these bones, trying to break them even as they grow. And if I could, I'd tell her that no matter how hard she tries, she'll never be able to chew the bones down to nothing.

Quicksand

THE FIRST TIME IT HAPPENED, Lana was standing in front of a shop window, trying to see past her reflection to the business inside. She doesn't remember anything special about the moment, but suddenly her insides were collapsing into themselves and the Styrofoam cup of coffee was pulled out of her hands and she dropped to her knees, gasping, everything around her taut and bright.

The feeling passed quickly, so quickly that for a moment she wondered if she'd imagined it. But as she straightened her body and wiped her clothes flat again, she looked for where she'd dropped her coffee and couldn't find it. Also missing: two buttons off her jacket and a single earring stud.

It happened again the next day, as she watched her clothes tumble inside the washer at the laundromat.

And the next, while she stood at the stove, stirring a pan of tomato sauce.

It always starts as a tingle in her chest, like static. A rushing sound in her ears. The skin beneath her collarbone shimmers and ripples like quicksand. Then, a flash of bone-deep cold and something close to her vanishes. A loose sock. A spatula. A moth. A copy of *The Hours*. A carton of berries. A tube of Neosporin.

Lana lives alone in a cold place, far away from anyone who used to know her. This town, this cold place, was once rich with lumber, its river teeming with logs being sent down to the sawmill to be manufactured. Victorian-style homes with gabled roofs and round turrets jeweled with stained glass windows were raised along the banks. The mountains were cleared of trees, and wealthy families flocked from the cities to purchase summer homes in the country.

Now, the river is quiet. The slumping turrets house bats, and the stained-glass windows are curtained with spiderwebs. Enough time has passed that a new forest has replaced the old. When Lana first moved to this town, she went on weekly walks through the woods, exploring the many trails that webbed the mountainside. Even though they were gone, replaced with invasive mulberries and cork and mimosa trees, she thought she could still sense the original hemlocks, the original beeches and oaks and birch. Their roots must still be underground, entangling with the new roots. A ghost forest knotted beneath the visible one, whispering secrets and warnings.

When her body started disappearing things around her, Lana increased her walks to four or five times a week. In the woods, alone, it's easy for her to imagine her affliction as a superpower. She tells herself she'll learn to control it. Use it for good. She'll swallow up hazardous waste, single-use plastic, oil spills, all those straws that get stuck in the nostrils and throats of sea creatures. She'll soak in the pesticides creeping through the soil from nearby farms. If she must consume, she'll consume the waste. She'll give her body to the good of the planet.

Lana practices. She makes-believe a training montage. She unzips her jacket to the cold and tries to feed her body small things she imagines it would want to open for. A turkey tail mushroom. A twig twisted up in lichen. An acorn. But her body never accepts the offerings. When she wants to become porous, her skin stays solid.

Then one day, Lana comes across a man.

It isn't unusual to pass other people in the woods. Miles of county-maintained trails cross the mountainside. What's odd is that, like her, the man isn't following a trail.

The creek is about twelve feet across. He's on one side. She's on the other.

She'd been crouching at the edge of the clear water, jacket open, trying to absorb cold creek pebbles into her skin. When she notices him on the opposite bank, she drops the pebbles. They make tiny splashes, and he looks up.

He's wearing a brown beanie and brown boots and a brown sweater. He has a soft chin and an untrimmed mustache that shrugs over his upper lip. He's carrying a metal detector.

The man smiles and raises a hand in greeting. "Hey." His tone is surprised, but friendly. He keeps his hand up, palm open, like he's aware he might come across as a threat.

At one time, Lana might have seen him as a danger. She would have calculated how long it would take him to cross the creek—it's too wide to jump across, but not too deep to wade through. In her past life, she would have avoided eye contact, would have kept her focus on his hands, aware of their potential energy, their ability to burst into movement like a mousetrap set to catch.

But now her body contains its own potential energy.

Lana zips up her jacket.

"What are you doing?" she asks him.

"I'm looking for buried things," he says. He switches on his metal detector and continues down the creek.

Lana follows on her side of the water, stepping over rot-softened logs and fists of moss.

Occasionally, the metal detector comes alive, beeping slowly and then frantically. The man pulls a little trowel out of his pocket and digs. Then, he holds up what he finds for Lana to see. First, he finds a nail. Then, a flattened beer can.

"Usually I don't find anything interesting," he says. He puts the can in a knapsack slung over his shoulder. "But I've gotten better and better at guessing where the good stuff might be."

Lana asks what he's looking for.

"I don't really know," he says. "The woods are full of all sorts of buried things."

She asks him to explain.

"Well, two hundred, three hundred years ago, European set- tlers built their homes in these woods. They're gone. But the stone foundations of their cabins are still here. And little pieces of their life they dropped or threw away."

Lana silently fills in the parts of the story he's left out. When those settlers first came to these woods, wolves and mountain cougars and martens still roamed. The settlers could hear them at night: howling just outside the ring of firelight, scratching at the edges of hens' coops, gnawing at the door to the ice house. These men weren't meant to be here, and they sensed it, so they transformed the woods into a place they could bear. They scarred over the old Susquehannock trails with wagon wheel tracks. They hunted the animals into eradication or drove them farther north. They cleared the dark forests with axes. Eventually it became inhospitable for them, too. Nothing left to hunt. No trees left to prevent erosion of their gardens. That was when they moved on.

When the creek narrows enough, Lana rock-hops across it, and now she and the man are on the same side. He keeps walking, sometimes bending down to dig a small hole or push around some rocks, and she follows.

She follows him all the way to the edge of the forest, into a clearing where a small house sits next to a one-lane road. "You can come in if you want to see some of the things I've found," he says.

She knows she should refuse, but she is feeling bold and curious.

The man's house has a hex sign over the front door: two intertwined bluebirds. Inside is small and dark, but clean. It gives her the same feeling the woods do. She wonders if, behind the drywall, there are beams hewn from the old forest, whispering to each other, expanding and contracting with the season's changes just as they did in life.

"What do you do for fun?" he asks as he pours her a glass of water from the tap.

"I don't really know anyone in town," Lana admits. "I guess I do what you do. Walk in the woods."

He shows her the collection of unburied treasure on his fireplace mantle. A bullet rattling around inside a crow's skull. A Union officer belt buckle with an eagle insignia. A lady's compact, rusted shut.

"I actually sell a lot of what I find," he says. "I have a booth at the antique store in town. You'd be surprised what people will pay for a little bit of history."

He bends over to pick up a jar of buttons, and she notices the tender, exposed back of his neck. As he straightens, he brushes her arm with his elbow. He quickly apologizes and takes a step back.

"I'm sorry. It's probably weird, me leading you back to my house like this."

She smiles. "I'm not afraid. I have a secret defense mechanism. If anyone tries to hurt me, my body will eat them up. Disappear them."

He laughs a little, and Lana takes a step closer.

He has a scar on his cheek. The eyelashes on his left eye are longer than the ones on his right eye. Lana hasn't been this close to another person in a very long time. The moment feels full of possibility. She's about to be brave, to close the space between them, when she feels that familiar tug between her clavicles. A cold pit piercing through her torso.

Lana shuts her eyes.

When she opens them, the man is gone. Lana clutches at her chest, gasping, but the skin is already solid.

"Hello?" she says to the empty house.

She checks the kitchen. Five boxes of Honey Nut Cheerios sit in a row on the counter. Three too-ripe bananas fill a white bowl. She checks the bathroom. She checks behind the shower curtain. She picks three damp hairs from the drain and holds them to her chest, like they might have the power to summon him back.

Lana wants to call out the man's name, but realizes she never asked for it.

Maybe he just stepped away, Lana thinks to herself. Any moment now, he'll be back.

She checks the bedroom. The bed is made, corners tucked in. Stacked cardboard boxes, turned sideways and filled with books, serve as a nightstand. She feels a heaviness in her chest she tries to ignore.

Below the bedroom window is a wire cage full of straw. A large, brown rabbit sits in the cage, staring at her unblinkingly. Its jaw moves in a circular motion, chewing a piece of straw. Its ears lie flat against its skull.

The room seems to tilt as Lana locks eyes with the rabbit. She steadies herself with a hand on the doorframe.

She realizes she's breathing too quickly. In fact, she can't catch her breath. She needs to be out of this house. She needs to be back in the woods.

Before Lana leaves, she grabs the house keys hanging from a hook next to the entrance. She locks the door behind her, and runs.

⁊

The next day, Lana tries to act normally. She goes to work in the downtown boutique that used to be a coffee shop. Before that it was a law office. Before that it was a courthouse. The boutique sells silk scarves and hand-dyed skirts and shapeless, linen dresses. All the drywall has been torn away to reveal old red bricks that are always cold to the touch, no matter what time of year.

Not many people come into the shop that day, so Lana spends most of her time folding and refolding piles of shirts, redoing each until it's perfect.

Her body keeps turning into quicksand, more often than usual. She's grateful business is slow, so no one notices when it swallows up a bobby-pin, a tank top left crumpled in the fitting room, a hazelnut creamer, and a bottle cap. She feels unmoored. When a customer taps on her shoulder, she quickly puts space between them, afraid she'll gulp them up, too. Nothing is off limits. Her insides feel sloshy. The deep cold that flashes through her body takes longer and longer to fade.

She can't stop thinking about the man. His mantlepiece treasures gathering dust. His family and friends who must realize he's missing. The rabbit closed inside its cage right now, chewing steadily through its pile of hay, the water in its dish getting shallow.

After work, she drives straight to the house in the woods, parking a quarter of a mile down the road to avoid suspicion if anyone comes looking for him.

In the mailbox there's a political ad addressed to Devon. She drops it in the trash bin next to the garage.

The house is just as she left it. The only thing that's changed is the rabbit. When she enters the bedroom, it's digging furiously at a corner of the cage, punching at the metal floor like it might eventually give way to dirt. Most of the straw has been kicked out between the bars, littering the carpet.

When the rabbit notices her, it stops. Freezes. Its eyes follow her as she searches the room.

Lana finds a container of rabbit kibble in the closet and drops some into the cage. She gathers as much of the straw as she can in her hands, and feeds it back between the bars. She refills the water dish using a paper cup she finds in the bathroom.

Lana watches the rabbit for a while—its brown fur scattered with lines of black and white to mimic the speckling of a forest floor, its spine forming a perfect arch. It looks like a regular rabbit, the type Lana sees in the woods, silent under a bush, ready to explode into motion. There's a leather string tied around its neck like a collar. She wonders if this rabbit was part of the man's collection. She imagines him digging the rabbit up from its underground burrow with a trowel when it was just a baby and placing it in his pocket, where it quivered like a beating heart. Or maybe he found it caught in a snare, leg broken. Maybe it was the runt of the litter, abandoned by its mother.

She reaches towards the cage, wanting to stroke the rabbit through the bars, to feel its small animal warmth against her knuckles.

Just as she's about to touch it, a word echoes through her mind: *No.*

It reverberates through her body. Her fingers tingle, and she recoils.

"Devon?" she says out loud.

Lana feels a shift inside her, like a release of atmospheric pressure.

"Devon, are you there?"

She likes parsley. There's some in the fridge. The words don't have a voice behind them, but they feel distinctly separate from her own stream of consciousness.

Lana walks to the fridge. Amongst bags of apples, milk past its due date, celery, and old take-out containers, she finds a plastic bag of wilted parsley.

Back in the bedroom, she drops the herbs into the cage. The rabbit nibbles them up quickly, efficiently.

"Where are you?" she says.

No one answers.

Lana wakes up on his couch, neck sore and back stiff.

The television is on. Two women, grinning at the camera in pencil skirts and blazers, arrange flowers in twin vases. The weather forecast scrolls by at the bottom of the screen.

She hadn't meant to fall asleep here. She had just sat down on the couch to think. But then her hand had found the television remote between the cushions as if she already knew where to find it. And she'd thought, what's the harm in resting my head?

She goes to the bathroom to splash her face with cold water and examines herself in the mirror. Her work clothes from yesterday are wrinkled and dark circles shadow her eyes.

Back in Devon's bedroom, she discards her own clothes and pulls on a plaid shirt she finds in his closet, followed by a pair of corduroy pants and high-ankle socks.

The clock shows that it's midmorning, and Lana knows it's time to leave for work.

But the thought of going into town, spending another shift sorting through clothes while she worries about the man her body has consumed, seems unbearable. She needs time to think, to figure out what to do next.

Suddenly, a phone rings.

Lana's hand goes to the phone in her pocket, but she already knows it's not her ringtone. She follows the sound through the house, until she finds a flip phone, lit up and vibrating, on the floor by Devon's bed.

The incoming call has a local area code, but it isn't labeled with a name. Not *Mom*, not *Dad*. Maybe it's just a spam. Or a reminder about an appointment.

"Who is it?" she asks, hoping Devon will respond, but her mind is silent.

When the phone stops ringing, Lana checks the recent call history. Other than this one, there are no recent missed calls and no voicemails. She doesn't go through texts. She knows now that to some degree Devon is in her, watching.

The call has shaken her. She doesn't want to go to work, but she also doesn't want to be caught in Devon's house if anyone shows up.

As she makes her way out of the house, she reaches for Devon's metal detector. Rather than heading toward the car, she goes to the woods.

The day is brisk and windy. Big clouds race across the sky, sporadically blocking out the sun. The branches, almost naked of leaves, clatter against each other. Lana can't hear any birdsong.

As Lana follows the familiar creek, she lets her mind go still. She can feel Devon's consciousness swimming beneath her own, and she lets it float closer to the surface. This man she absorbed; he doesn't think about polar bears' shrinking habitat. He doesn't think about glaciers chewed away by heat waves, or how light pollution is throwing migrating birds off course. He doesn't think about the people and animals the town's founders killed or displaced. Devon thinks of old, buried things. He notices where the trees grow in a row and wonders if, two hundred years ago, they marked the edge of a schoolyard, if maybe the students helped to plant them. He wonders what it'd be like to find a wolf print in the mud, or to come across it with its snout bent to the creek, pink tongue scooping water between its pointed teeth.

Once or twice the metal detector beeps, but each time Lana kicks around in the dirt, she finds only a bit of trash or a crusty penny. The ground becomes steeper, and the detector beeps less frequently. Lana's not familiar with this part of the forest. The trees are younger here. They're tall, but thin-trunked from racing each other toward the light. This patch of forest must have been the last to be cleared by lumber companies.

As Lana crests the hill, she hears a gunshot crack and echo through the valley.

A few moments later, a gray-haired man in a camo jacket and bright orange vest walks across the creek a few yards ahead of her. A dead rabbit swings from one hand. A long-barreled gun is in the other.

The man stops mid-creek and raises the hand holding the rabbit in familiarity. Then he pauses and squints at Lana.

"Sorry," he says. "I thought..." He drops his hand. "You're on game land. Shouldn't be out here during hunting season."

"Sorry," she says.

The hunter stares at her.

"You need help getting back? You're pretty far off trail."

Lana's chest tightens. "I'm fine," she says.

She waits until the hunter has disappeared back into the forest before turning around. She follows the creek downhill, using the metal detector as a cane.

She hadn't paid attention to how long she'd been walking. Fifteen minutes go by, then twenty, and she still hasn't returned to a familiar part of the forest.

The sky has become overcast, the forest dim despite the day still being young. A crow caws once somewhere close by, but she doesn't see it in the branches.

Something crashes through the bushes on the other side of the creek. Lana thinks it must be a deer, and when she looks, she sees the hunter.

He's among the trees, about a hundred feet away, his orange vest no longer draped around his shoulders. In his camo jacket, he's the same color as the forest.

He's standing motionless.

His back is to her.

Lana gasps. She stumbles over some rocks and runs in opposite direction, away from the creek and into the woods. Fear pulses in her chest like a trapped, wild bird.

She runs, dodging prickly bushes and leaping over logs.

A gunshot cracks through the trees, and the crow caws wildly.

Ahead of her, Lana can see a wall. Well, the shape of a wall, dressed in green moss and brown lichen. She scurries behind it and presses her back against the stone.

A family once lived here. The thought is flotsam, catching in her mind. *Maybe they had a son and daughter. Some chickens that lay brown eggs.*

She closes her eyes and breathes. She tells herself the hunter didn't mean to follow her. She tells herself he's just hunting game. He's not hunting her.

Lana counts to two hundred, then stands up. She walks downhill through the underbrush until she finds a trail. She forces herself not to act like prey, not to run.

⅋

When Lana was young, there was no forest for her to play in. But there was an empty lot next to her house. Machines had cut a rectangular, six-foot deep hole in the earth in preparation to build a house's foundation. But the project had been abandoned. The freshly cleared lot grew over with wild sumac. With every rain and every melting snowfall, the hole eroded a little bit back into itself.

Lana wasn't allowed to play in the empty lot, but she would go there anyway.

She'd slide down into the hole, and make believe that it was her home. She used a stick to carve shelves into the walls. She laid down rocks to mark the edges of the rooms. Here was her kitchen. There was her bedroom. She piled dirt into the shape of a pillow and lay back, looking at the rectangle of sky above her. She'd see a plane pass overhead and imagine that she and the people in that plane were the only humans left on Earth.

Once, while she was playing in the hole, it started to rain. It had been raining on and off all week, and the ground was already slippery and soft. When Lana tried to climb out, her feet couldn't find a grip. The more she tried, the slicker the sides of the hole became.

Lana considered screaming, but was more afraid of her parents than she was of the rain. She took off her shoes, which had started making a gulping sound whenever she tried lifting them from the sticky pit of mud forming around her.

Eventually, she pulled herself out. She used the shelves she'd carved as footholds. She let herself be washed clean in the rain. The next day, when the puddles had dried, she went back in.

⅋

That night, Lana dreams of the old forest. An untouched pocket where there are still Eastern hemlocks with pinecones as delicate as flowers. Beech trees with smooth, gray trunks like the ankles of giants. Black gum trees. Red maple. Northern red oak. Black birch. Yellow birch. Turkey tail mushrooms that grow on trunks high into the canopy.

When she wakes, she knows the dream didn't belong to her. It belonged to Devon. Her own dreams are often dystopian, filled with anxiety, with lost things.

Two days have passed, and no one has come looking for him. Lana knows, because she hasn't left his house. Even his phone remains silent.

Lana's phone, on the other hand, lights up with texts from her coworkers and eventually her boss. She replies that she's sick, that she's sorry, but she'll be back in a few days.

Lana eats through the food in Devon's fridge. She watches the television programs she can sense he likes. Her body sucks up a safety pin, a spoon, and a bar of soap.

Every now and then, Devon says something.

The brass buckle needs shining.

It's time to bury the tulip bulbs.

It never feels like he's speaking to her, though. It feels like he's speaking to himself, like he doesn't realize he's not fully here.

On the fourth day, she goes an hour before she remembers who she is. She eats two hard-boiled eggs. She drinks coffee black, even though it gives her a stomachache. She thinks about how she needs to restock her antique booth next week. She's about to put on her shoes and step outside, when she comes back into herself.

Her body feels cool and prickly, like it does after she's become quicksand. Though it doesn't appear that she's vanished anything.

Her phone is ringing in her pocket.

"Hello," she says, without checking the number first.

"Hey Lana. Are you on your way?"

Shit. She was supposed to be back at work today.

"Oh," she says. "I'm sorry. I was on my way. But I, I think I'm still too sick."

There's a pause on the other end. "Get better. But you've got to let us know when this happens. Don't wait for us to call you."

Lana sits on the bed and drops her phone on the blanket next to her. She needs to find a way get Devon out. But how? She's only ever consumed, not expelled. Lana can't focus. The rabbit is chewing loudly on the bars of the cage, and the sound of tooth on metal pierces through her.

The first time Devon spoke, it was when she'd almost touched his rabbit. She'd been reaching out to touch it, and he had stopped her. Maybe it's also the key to getting him out. She looks at the rabbit with its quivering nose, shaped like a perfect Y stitch. Its black eyes reflect her face back to herself.

❧

Since her encounter with the hunter, Lana hasn't entered the forest. But today, she walks slowly to its edge, where mowed grass transitions into brush.

The rabbit is limp and docile in her arms. Lana is surprised by its weight, by the distinct patter of its heart, palpable even through fabric. She holds it to her chest, swaddling it in her flannel shirt.

It's that time when day tips towards night, and everything begins to lose its color.

She takes a deep breath, like she's about to cast an incantation.

"Devon," she says out loud, "I'm going to let it go."

She crouches down to the grass, to show that she means business.

"Unless you stop me, Devon. You better come out and stop me."

Lana doesn't anticipate the strength of the rabbit's legs. As she rests its paws on the ground, it becomes suddenly agile. It kicks out of her hands and bounds into forest, running loudly through the underbrush.

"No," she calls after it, like it might respond.

She hadn't meant to let the rabbit go, not really. She thought just the threat of releasing it might shake Devon loose.

And to a degree, it seems to have worked. Suddenly, Devon is thrashing inside her. *Go after her. Go.*

Lana listens. She sprints into the woods.

She can't believe it when, almost immediately, she spots the rabbit poised next to a log. Maybe it's disoriented, unsure of what to do now that it's faced with an entire, open forest. Lana slows to a tiptoe. The rabbit's nose twitches. Its ears are fully erect. They turn, scanning the forest.

Just as she thinks she'll do it, she'll catch the rabbit, it bursts again into motion. Lana follows it down a hill, through a patch of mountain laurels. The forest is growing even darker, and she imagines the sun, hiding behind the clouds, balanced on the horizon. Lana thinks about turning back, but Devon's thoughts spur her on: *Go. Go. She's not safe alone out here.*

Lana is in a narrow valley now, and here the trees are larger than what she's used to, their trunks thicker. The names of the trees come to her as she sees them. Old growth trees.

"Where am I?" she says.

Her foot catches on a root, and she falls, skinning her knees and scraping up her palms.

Devon is not coming out. She sees that now.

Lana gets back to her feet. She tries to brush the dirt off her hands, but that just pushes it deeper into her cuts.

Maybe there's an option she didn't consider. Instead of pushing him out, she could let Devon take the reins. It'd be easy to slip into his life; she could manage his antique booth, take over his role of treasure hunter. Instead of spending her days thinking about the ways humans' choices of the past and present have doomed the planet, Lana could focus on this small patch of forest. She could replace her own memories with Devon's. As invasive as it's been to have his thoughts floating through her, it's also been freeing. The world is simpler in his eyes. Maybe, with him in charge, she'd stop becoming quicksand. She could be normal, or closer to it.

As Lana reaches a clearing, she spots the rabbit huddling at the base of a laurel shrub. She takes slow steps forward, but as she gets closer, she realizes it can't run away. The string of leather around its neck has caught on the shrub.

The forest floor ripples with roots just beneath the surface. Lana sits down on the root of an oak that has broken through the soil and carefully reaches for the string. She tries first to untie it, but the rabbit flails at her touch, twisting the string so that it tightens around its neck.

Lana withdraws her hands. She wishes she could see inside the rabbit to its olive-size heart and speak to it in a way that it would understand, tell it that she will not hurt it. That it will be okay.

In the clearing to her right, someone has made a firepit ringed in flattened beer cans. Overhead, an airliner draws a line of chemtrails across the darkening sky. She imagines what the people inside see out the windows. A small square of forest with clean borders, surrounded by a patchwork quilt of crops threaded with roads. When the sun disappears, the cities will still be visible: snow globes of light in the dark.

The rabbit has calmed. Lana reaches again for the string. She knows the rabbit will dash off again the moment she frees it. Its paws will instinctively find their way through the underbrush, knowing which routes will be safe.

Devon knows it too. *Grab her now. This is your...*

But she interrupts him. She shushes him quiet.

As she unties the knot, she feels her chest open. Feels herself becoming porous. And this time, it doesn't stop at her chest. The feeling spreads down her ribcage to her pelvis, to her knees. To her wrists. To her feet and hands. She breathes in the waning, muted sunlight. The turkey tail mushrooms climbing the tree like steps into the canopy. The carbon dioxide in the air. The pesticides creeping through the soil from nearby farms.

She lets it filter right through her.

We Left

ON SATURDAY MORNING, we left the desert for the mountains. Four of us packed into Libby's old pick-up truck that chugged up the steep, one lane road. A minivan rode our bumper, aching to pass us, but Libby wouldn't pull over. "Goodbye, cactus," we said to the last saguaro. "Goodbye, ocotillo," we said to the last ocotillo. "Goodbye, oaks," we said to the last scraggly, blue oaks. Then, like magic, we were surrounded by forest.

We rolled down the windows and swallowed the pine-infused air, twenty degrees cooler than the desert city below. They called this mountain a sky island. It erupted from the desert, stacking one habitat on top of another. At the tippy top, spruce fir forests dropped pinecones, and dragonflies swarmed over slow, shallow streams. Moss blushed in the shadows.

We sang along with the crackling radio until the station went out altogether, the signal lost amongst trees and buttes and mountain valleys. The turn for the cabin came up abruptly, obscured by a patch of aspen. "Red mailbox!" Iris shouted. "There it is!" Libby hit the brake and did a tight turn onto the dirt road. The car behind us laid on the horn and Libby flipped the driver the bird through the window.

We followed the narrow road through the woods, dust kicking up behind us like a trailing cape. After ten minutes, we reached the cabin. It was a new build, all glossy pine and big windows that reflected the trees and blue sky. We recognized Joan's car in the driveway, with its COEXIST and MY CAT MADE THE HONOR ROLL bumper stickers.

We unloaded our suitcases from the bed of the truck, swaying slightly. The air felt different at 8,000 feet above the desert. Our blood moved differently in our veins.

As we lingered on the driveway, Nadya said, "If it gets weird, we can just leave, right?"

"It's only a weekend," Val reminded her. "But sure. We can have a code word. If it gets too cringe for you, just slip 'avocado' into casual conversation."

"I can see Joan in the window," Iris warned. "She's waiting for us. Come on."

We hoisted our bags off the ground and made our way to the porch. Before any of us could raise a fist to knock, the door swung open. Joan stood in the foyer, grinning, her arms outstretched.

"Welcome to the first Annual Retreat for Girls with Beastly Boyfriends," she said. "I'm so pleased to see you."

Joan pulled us into a perfumed group hug, and we winced at each other over her shoulders.

"Pleased to see you, too," Val said. We nodded, trying to look as earnest as possible.

⁂

We—Val, Iris, Nadya, and Libby—had met only two months ago, though it felt like much longer.

On a Sunday in late winter, we arrived separately at a park in midtown Tucson. We each clutched a little slip of paper we'd ripped off a flier found on a phone pole. The flier, in Chiller font, had sported the words: *Support Group for Girls with Beastly Boyfriends. Is your partner a monster-skinned humanoid? Does your boo have fangs, feathers, or fur?*

Commiserate with like-minded women. And beneath that: *Not a Joke. Serious Participants Only.*

The flier had told us to meet under the big acacia tree. To look for the lady with the wolf blanket.

The blanket was unmissable. It featured a large, howling, gray wolf superimposed against the aurora borealis. The sort of blanket you'd find at a truck stop giftshop. We weren't sure who we expected to go with that blanket, but it was not Joan. She had long, manicured nails and stiff hair, sprayed into a perfect bob. She wore a linen, buttoned up blouse and pencil skirt and had a vibe we associated with realtors. She smiled widely, with perfectly straight teeth, and indicated for us each to sit on a different corner of the blanket.

We eyed each other. We were all in our mid to late twenties. We wore baggy jeans and ball caps, or leggings and crop tops. We dressed like we were ready to run. When we smiled politely at each other, we were sure not to make eye contact for too long.

"Well," Joan said, clapping her hands together. "Don't be shy. Let's introduce ourselves. Say your name and creature type."

We grimaced at her use of the phrase "creature type." It made us feel like we were part of a role-playing game, like she was about to pass out costumes and props and have us act out our relationships.

Val cleared her throat. She muttered that she was dating a vampire.

Iris: a merman.

Libby: a werewolf.

Nadya: a ghost. "Though I'm not sure that counts as a *beastly* boyfriend," she added.

"I won't turn you away for it," Joan said with a little laugh. She cleared her throat. "I myself had a fling with a minotaur in the early '90s. I met him on a study abroad trip to Greece. So, I know how you all feel. Relationships with men of the mythic variety can be intense." She reddened suddenly. "But there will always be a power imbalance. We are not here to judge each other's relationships, but to support each other. As women. To remind each other that we are powerful, too."

We eyed each other, watching for reactions. We kept our faces blank.

At the end of the session, Joan gave us each an assignment to create our fifty-year plans. "I know, it's hard to imagine living so long. You're used to being close to danger. But you've got to stop living in the present. It's time to think about your futures."

Despite our mild embarrassment, we all showed up on the following Sunday. This time, we smiled openly at the sight of each other.

"I was afraid I'd be the only one to show up," Iris whispered as Joan spread out the blanket.

Val told us her fifty-year plan included going to law school. She wanted to be an immigration lawyer and help people like her parents, who'd immigrated from Belize when they were her age. "Then, at age sixty-five, I'll retire," she said. "I'll sell my house and move abroad. Somewhere near a beach."

Libby's plan was to buy some land up north. "Maybe have a little farm. A few goats, a cow. Chickens. Some hardy crops that will weather climate collapse."

Iris wanted to go back to school for visual art. "And I know this will sound so traditional, so don't laugh. But I think my ideal job would be having a couple kids and staying home to raise them. I could make art in my spare time."

Nadya said she wasn't sure what she wanted to be, but she'd like to travel. She'd like to get out of debt. She thought it'd be nice to foster old dogs from the shelter that no one else wanted.

"I notice that none of you included your boyfriends in these plans," Joan said, looking around the circle meaningfully when we'd finished.

"I didn't know we were allowed to include them," Nadya said.

Joan ignored her. "How would your boyfriends fit into these wonderful plans you've made for your futures? That's it for today, but I want you to think on that."

While Joan stayed behind to fold the wolf blanket into a tote bag, we wandered back to the parking lot. We stood next to our cars, fingering our keys, putting off leaving.

Val was the one to finally suggest we go out for coffee.

We went to a café down the road and crowded around a small table in the upstairs loft. It was one of those places where the music is always too loud, the space too warm with the heat of espresso machines and coffee grinders and steamers constantly running. Our knees bumped under the table. The caffeine in our iced mochas made our brains feel like rubber bands.

"So," Nadya said, imitating Joan's breathiness, "do you all feel like strong, independent women now?"

We smiled. We let our postures shift. We'd shared the broad strokes of our relationships in the support group, but now we said what we couldn't, wouldn't, say in front of Joan.

We'd met our boyfriends when we were teenagers. We met them at prom, in chemistry class, at a bonfire in the Catalinas, in the haunted hotel our parents dragged us to on summer vacation. We spent our high school years getting caught up in millennia-old monster clan disputes. We became accessories to crimes while covering up our boyfriend's accidental nocturnal murders. We were kidnapped by rival monsters as part of convoluted revenge plots. We lived in constant fear that one day some neighborhood busybody would post security cam footage of our boyfriends clawing/stalking/floating on Nextdoor, and a top-secret governmental research group would come take our boyfriends away. The details of our stories were different, but they shared a template.

Now, we were in our twenties. We had bachelor's degrees and jobs.

No one bothered to kidnap us anymore, which was a relief. But also a little insulting. It reminded us that we were no longer teenagers. We had flab hanging from our upper arms. We had early-onset wrinkles caused by sun damage and a decade of worrying. We were learning about retirement funds. The sexy Italian vampire clans weren't interested in holding *us* hostage.

Libby complained of matted fur in the shower that clogged her drains—"Why can't he just wipe up after himself?" She complained that on the full moon, he'd come home with bird bones stuck between his teeth, cactus quills through his lips.

Val complained that her boyfriend never visibly aged. She used to beg him to turn her into a vampire, so they could be immortal together, but he always said no. Maybe he regretted it now. Sometimes he'd point out an ad for retinoid creams and say, "I wonder if that really works." The other day he plucked a silver hair from her head without asking.

Her response was to suggest that maybe he put some streaks of gray in his own hair, so they'd stop getting weird looks at bars.

We sipped at our drinks even after they were gone and all that was left was the melting ice.

After that day, we made it our habit to get coffee following every Sunday support group. We'd do Joan's exercises and write letters to our past and future selves or draw pictures of our inner child. And then we'd go to the café and talk about what really bothered us.

Iris told us that her boyfriend spent half the year deep in the Mid-Pacific to be with his family and deal with merperson business. At the end of the summer, she'd go to a specific isolated beach near San Diego and wait for him to emerge from the waves and transform back into a man. She couldn't text him while he was gone, couldn't write letters. Every summer, she worried he wouldn't return to her.

We asked Nadya what it was like to date a ghost. She said that looking at him was like trying to hold onto someone you'd seen in a dream. He floated through objects. His edges blurred and shimmered. He couldn't hold her hand, couldn't kiss her.

We imagined never being touched. Never being able to hold our boyfriend's hand or smell his hair. To never feel the damp of morning dew on his skin or count the vertebrae on his back with our fingers.

"That doesn't really bother me," Nadya responded, shrugging. "I never really cared about that part anyway."

After five consecutive weeks of meeting in the park, Joan brought up the idea of a retreat.

"We've made great progress," she said, "I think we're ready now to really dive in. To give ourselves the space to just focus on ourselves. We deserve that, don't we?"

We looked at each other and shrugged. As corny as we found our support group meetings to be, we valued them for bringing us together. We'd gotten close, but none of us had had much luck with long-term friendships. We weren't sure that our new friendship would last without the scaffolding our Sunday meetings provided.

"Terrific," Joan said, taking our silence as agreement. "This will be so much fun."

Though we knew the main road was just a short drive away, the cabin had the feeling of being in the middle of nowhere. Any other houses or roads were obscured by boulders or hills or trees. When Joan walked us to the back patio, all we could hear was the cackle of jays and the soft whisper of wind rustling pine needles. No distant thrum of traffic. Not even the low roar of a plane cutting across the sky.

"Can you believe I found this place on the internet?" Joan said. "The owner said it's usually booked up. We're lucky it was open this weekend."

The cabin was open concept, with the kitchen and living space all connected in one large high-ceilinged room. But there was a short hallway in the back that led to three bedrooms and a cramped bathroom.

Joan led us to a bedroom with two bunkbeds. It was clearly set up to be the kids' room on family vacations. The bedspreads featured princesses and heavy machinery and cartoonish sea creatures. A nightlight shaped like a smiling sun lay on the floor next to an outlet.

Joan left us to unpack, but we just flopped onto the lower bunks.

"So, what did you tell your boyfriends you were doing this weekend?" Nadya asked.

"Mine already left for the Pacific," Iris said.

"I told him I was staying at a cabin with friends," Val said. "He's just relieved to hear I've made some human friends."

"Same," Nadya and Libby said, nodding.

None of us had mentioned to our boyfriends that we'd joined a support group. As much as they annoyed us, we knew they already carried the guilt of past injuries, past dramas. It'd hurt their feelings to know we needed counseling to deal with their existences.

That evening we sat at the round dining table while Joan placed bowls of chili and salad in front of us. After we cleared our plates, she gave us each a blank sheet of paper and directed us to draw two large, intersecting circles.

"We're going to make Venn diagrams," she explained. "On the right side, we'll write the qualities of our ideal partner. On the left, we'll list the qualities of our current partner. In the middle, we'll see if there are any ways those two sides overlap."

She turned on a fake battery-operated candle and placed it in the center of the table for ambience. After fifteen or so minutes of eating and writing quietly, she asked us to share our Venn diagrams, and we reluctantly put our pencils to the side.

Joan picked up Libby's and read it thoughtfully. "So, you like that your boyfriend is outdoorsy, like you are, and that he—" She paused and read verbatim, "has nice muscles."

Val snorted, and Joan glanced at her, looking more confused than annoyed.

She moved on to Nadya's. "Your ideal partner is someone who could enjoy your hobbies. You also wish he was someone you could introduce to your family. I'm sure it's very difficult, not being able to share your love with others."

Nadya looked away. "It's fine, I guess."

As Joan reached for Val's paper, Val grabbed it and folded it into quarters. She stuffed it in one of her pockets. "Thanks, Joan, but I think I'm good. I'm feeling pretty tired. Do you mind if I turn in for the night?"

Joan seemed disappointed, but nodded. It was still early in the evening, but she suggested that maybe we all get ready for bed and continue in the morning. "I have a surprise that I think you'll enjoy," she said, smiling mysteriously.

After each taking our turn in the single bathroom, we climbed into our narrow beds, plugged in the nightlight, and whispered into the half-dark.

"Did you know the moon is moving away from Earth?" Libby asked. "I just read that somewhere. An inch a year. Hypothetically, if it moved far enough away, do you think he'd stop changing on the full moon?"

"Would you want that?"

She didn't answer, but we imagined her shrugging in the dark. We'd all imagined, at some point, what it'd be like if our boyfriends could become—or stay—human. But that wasn't a thought we liked to dwell on.

❧

We woke to pans clashing and the soft murmur of voices down the hall. In our pajamas, our oversized T-shirts, our basketball shorts, brushing hair from our eyes, we wandered into the main room.

"What the," Libby said.

Four men sat around the table, pancakes and eggs piled high on their plates. Mugs of coffee were clutched between their hands.

Iris tried reversing us back into the bedroom, but it was too late.

"Surprise!" Joan said. "Come on, don't be shy. Meet our guests."

The table was not built for nine people, but Joan had pulled in some of the patio chairs. She arranged us so that we were split up, each sitting next to a guy. We brushed our tangled hair with our fingers and adjusted our shirts self-consciously. The men nodded and said, "Hey." They were all spectacularly normal looking. Twenty-somethings in khaki shorts with neat haircuts. As soon as we entered the room, their chatter had stopped. They looked as unsure as we did.

Val turned to Joan, "What is going on?"

Joan set food on our plates and poured syrup over our pancakes without asking us to say "when." After we'd all been served, she stood at the head of the table. "Girls, I'd like you to meet the Boys with Ghastly Girlfriends. Who wants a mimosa?"

We stared at each other, open-mouthed.

Joan prompted the men to introduce themselves as she poured orange juice and champagne into stemmed glasses. We learned that Greg was dating a nymph. Gabriel: a selkie. Alexander: a siren. Louis: a banshee.

"Sorry," Gabriel said, leaning in and whispering as Joan dug for ice in the fridge. "She said you were expecting us."

"I wish I had some avocado on these eggs," Nadya said pointedly. "Like, right now."

"Sorry, no avocados," Joan said. "I have spinach, though. Holler if you want any. Now don't be shy, gals. I think you'll find that you all have a lot in common." She winked at us. "Think about those Venn diagrams, ladies."

"What Venn diagrams?" Louis asked.

We sat in silence, filling our mouths with pancakes to avoid having to speak. The morning sun streamed through the east-facing windows, surrounding us in a square of light. We squinted at our breakfasts.

We rushed into our bedroom the moment we'd finished eating.

"We're leaving, right?" Nadya hissed as we changed into shorts and T-shirts. "She's trying to set us up with these randos. I think that's a step too far."

"Yes, it's awkward, but I don't want to be rude," Iris said. "She means well. She is the one who brought us together, right?"

"Let's just try to make it through the day," Val said. "Can you do that?"

Nadya glared, but nodded.

Next on Joan's schedule was a group hike. She loaded our daypacks up with trail mix and fruit and sandwiches and extra water, then led us to a narrow trail at the edge of the property. Apparently, it linked up to a more popular trail a couple miles into the woods.

Up the mountain we went. The day was already warm, but we could still feel ribbons of cold rising from the valleys when we walked through a dip in the terrain.

Though we all grew up in the city at the base of the mountain, Libby was the only one who had spent much time hiking here. The rest of us had mostly only come to visit the little village at the top of the mountain. In the summer, our parents would drive us up for a respite from the heat. We'd sit in our swimsuits in the stream, or we'd buy giant cookies from the Cookie Cabin with a scoop of vanilla ice cream on top. In the winter we'd come up to ski on the north side of the mountain. None of us were familiar with this trail.

We tried to hang behind the group, but the men kept slowing their pace to match ours. They wanted to know how we'd met our boyfriends, how long we'd been together, how we handled our partners' "dark sides." We almost felt bad for them. They seemed so desperate for answers.

"Joan," Nadya called eventually. "I have to pee."

The group stopped. "Uh," Joan said. "You'll have to go in the woods."

"I know," Nadya responded. "Don't look! You guys keep walking. The girls will stay with me, and we'll catch up in a minute."

"Sure. Of course."

The boys shuffled forward, and we waited on the trail until they disappeared around a bend.

"Do you really have to go?" Iris asked. "Or are you just trying to separate us?"

"Can't it be both?" Nadya asked. "Now help me find something to pee behind. I don't want some other hiker seeing me, either."

This part of the forest didn't have much ground cover. Any bushes or walls of fern had been cleared by past fires. We could see the black, shiny scars on the sides of the trees. We had to walk a few minutes off trail before we found a patch of boulders that Nadya found acceptable.

We'd barely turned our backs to her, when Nadya shouted out. It was followed by the sound of snapping twigs and a thump.

Behind the boulders was a twenty-foot steep incline of dead leaves and old brush and protruding roots. Nadya lay at the bottom, clutching her ankle.

"I'm such an idiot," she called up. "I lost my balance. Go get Joan and the guys."

"No way," Val said. "We're not leaving you down there."

We slid down the bank, trying to control our slide by holding roots and rocks where we could. When we reached the bottom, we saw that Nadya's right ankle had already begun to swell under her sock.

"It's nothing," she said. "I've felt worse."

But she looked pale, and when she tried to stand, she groaned and fell back to the ground. We removed her shoe and thick hiking sock, and then put the sock back on. Was compressing the ankle a good or bad thing? None of us could remember.

We looked around ourselves desperately, as though we'd find the answer sitting on the ground. Nadya had tumbled into a narrow gully. It felt at least ten degrees cooler here than it had been up on the trail.

"Look," Libby said.

A few yards away, hidden in shadow-soaked patch of trees, there was a small cabin. It had dark brown wood siding. The window and doorframes were painted white, though the color was chipping. A few shingles were missing from the roof. The narrow windows were curtained in spiderwebs. It was a stark difference from the cabin Joan had rented.

"It must be an old forest ranger cabin," said Libby.

"Come on, let's get you off the ground," Val said.

Val and Libby propped Nadya up and half-carried her to the cabin. Iris went ahead and tried the knob. As the door swung open, there was the sound of small creatures skittering out of sight in the dark corners. The cabin was mostly empty, except for a single card table, a cupboard built into the wall over a sink, and two narrow twin beds with missing mattresses. A topographical map of the mountain was pinned to the wall, edges curling.

We lowered Nadya onto the floor and made a stack out of our backpacks for her to elevate her ankle.

Iris took her phone out of her pocket.

"No service. No bars," she said.

The rest of us took out our phones and confirmed that it was the same for us.

We sat cross-legged on the dusty floor. Needled branches scraped against the roof, and a woodpecker tapped against one of the outdoor vents.

"Joan and the guys can't be very far ahead," Val said. "I can go get them now, if you want."

"No," Nadya said, shaking her head. "I changed my mind. Let's just stay here awhile. I just need to rest, then I'll be okay."

"They're probably starting to —" Iris began, but Nadya cut her off.

"It's fine. They'll assume we ditched and went back to the cabin. I mean, the big cabin. It's nice here. Let's just appreciate the quiet."

She lay back on the floor, closing her eyes. Iris adjusted the bags under her ankle, and Nadya grimaced, but didn't say anything. Eventually, her breathing slowed, and she appeared to slip into a shallow sleep.

To pass the time while Nadya slept, we took an inventory of everything we could find in the cabin. Libby found a matchbox, but when she slid it open, it was full of burnt stubs and cigarette butts. Iris found a can opener. Val found a paperback western with curling pages. Val turned the knobs on the sink, and the pipes coughed up a trickle of brown liquid. Then nothing.

As we explored the cabin, clouds began to build in the previously blue sky. When we heard the first rumbles of thunder, we woke Nadya. We all knew how quickly storms could build in the summer. From our homes in the desert, we'd see them collect over the mountains as the city remained dry within a bubble of heat.

"I think it's time to go," Iris whispered to Nadya gently.

But Nadya's ankle seemed even worse than before. Purple and blue bruises spread under her skin like watercolors, and by the time we got her up, leaning on our shoulders, big drops of rain had already started to splatter against the roof of the cabin.

We settled back on the floor. We kept the door open and watched as the rain transformed from a sprinkle into a downpour. The intoxicating smell of precipitation rolled over us in waves as our gully transformed into a body of water. Rainwater streamed down the steep banks, pooled around the edges of the cabin. Pine needles floated and swirled in the uneven current.

We moved onto one of the twin beds as the water began to seep over the door frame and creep across the floor.

"No closer," we whispered to the water, as it spread throughout the cabin. "That's close enough." And maybe our pleading worked, because the flood never rose above the very base of the bedframe.

By the time the rain stopped and the water began to recede—swallowed up by thirsty roots and draining into lower crevices of the mountain—the sun had gone down. We didn't notice the sun setting. Suddenly, it was just dark. We felt our way through the cabin, using our shoes to sweep any remaining water towards the door. Then we swung the door shut. We ate the peanut butter and jelly sandwiches we'd packed that morning. We peeled oranges and dropped the peels on the damp floor.

There was nothing to do but sit. We agreed that in the dark, with Nadya's hurt ankle, it was too risky to attempt climbing the water-logged banks.

To fill the silence, Iris said, "In primary school, my school would take us on field trips up the mountain." She described how they'd stop at the big overlook, the one with enough space for a school bus to both park and turn around. The teachers would give the kids crayons and paper and tell them to make bark and stone rubbings. A park ranger told them that you could find creatures here, on this sky island, that would never been seen in the desert below. Black bears. Foxes. Coatimundis. Species that were trapped at the top after the last Ice Age. The desert might as well be a sea.

Now, sitting in the dark cabin, we wondered what other strangeness evolved here since the cold retreated and the land below turned to desert. What was hiding in the fire-scarred forests that the forest rangers didn't talk about—or know about?

As the night grew colder, we moved closer together on the bed. We pulled our knees into our shirts and surrounded ourselves with our backpacks to hold in the warmth. We let Nadya lie down with her ankle resting on our laps. The rest of us fell asleep sitting up.

We were startled awake by a knock at the door.

It was late. How late, we didn't know. The room was pitch black.

"Maybe it's Joan," Nadya whispered.

We held our breaths, waiting to see if we'd imagined it. Waiting to see if it had just been the wind shaking the windows or a fallen branch clattering onto the roof.

But then there it was again. Three hard taps that rattled the door in its frame.

We slapped our hands over our mouths to stifle our yelps.

"If it's Joan, why isn't she calling for us?" Nadya whispered. "Why don't we see a flashlight? I don't hear any of the guys with her."

It was true. Through the windows, we saw no beam of light. We heard no chatter of voices.

We felt Libby shift next to us. We tried to hold her back, but she pulled away. She shuffled through the darkness for a few seconds, and then there was the scrape of the card table being pushed across the cabin floor. The thump of the table colliding with the wall.

She slid back onto the bed.

"Now they know we're in here," Nadya hissed.

"I jammed the table under the door knob. We're safe," she said.

It was just then that the door shook again, this time like someone had taken hold of it and was trying to pull it from its hinges.

"Where are you?" The voice cut through the cabin like a cold frost. "Where are my powerful women? Where have you gone?"

We inhaled collectively.

It was Joan's voice, though it sounded different than we remembered. It sounded like a rusty hinge. Like a branch scraping a window.

"I've been looking for you," she said.

The voice circled us, circled the cabin.

We leaned into each other on the bottom bunk, hands finding each other's hands.

"What *is* she?" Iris whispered.

This was the point at which our boyfriends usually emerged from the shadows to save us.

Iris thought of the time she was dragged from her kayak by an envious mermaid and her boyfriend had had to squeeze the sea out her lungs before she could breathe again. Val thought of the time she was kidnapped by a Romanian vampire prince and held hostage in an empty office building until her boyfriend tracked her down. Nadya thought of the poltergeist that lived in her attic until her boyfriend spirited him away. Libby thought of the time she got caught in a werewolf hunter's trap, and when the hunter came to collect, her boyfriend hit him and hit him until he stopped fighting back and Libby was afraid to look to see what happened afterwards.

But we weren't on our boyfriends' minds tonight. They were doing normal, boyfriend things. They were playing Call of Duty. They were finishing up the last of our edibles. They were flipping through magazines, thinking of women that weren't us.

We had relied on our boyfriends' magic for too long. What good was it now?

"You think you're better than me." The voice breathed through the cracks in the walls, crawled up our necks. "You think I don't see your condescending smiles, your sideways glances at each other. You think I don't know you're trying to leave me, after all I've done?"

"Nadya?" The voice seemed to come from the roof now. We heard footsteps above us, heavy thumps.

"No," Nadya said, quietly.

"Libby?"

"No." We all said it this time, quietly.

"Val? Iris?"

"No! No!" We chanted it. Quietly at first. Then we let our voices get louder and louder. "No. No. No." This could be our magic word, our seal of protection. We let the word grow ragged and sharp in our throats. *No.*

We chanted for minutes or maybe hours.

When our voices finally grew hoarse and our lungs had nothing left to give, we stopped. The forest was silent around us. Not even a wind rattled the doors and windows. We wrapped our arms around each other and felt the warmth, the beating hearts, the blood moving through veins.

The next day, we didn't leave the gully. Instead, we spent our time cleaning up the cabin, sweeping away the debris that had floated in with the flood. We used branches to dig ditches that could redirect the waters, should a downpour come again. We dug up cold mud to press on Nadya's ankle.

As we worked, we planned.

"We'll go into the village, just once, to get supplies. But then we'll learn to brew pine needle tea. We'll learn to trap squirrels and forage for mushrooms."

"We'll make Nadya a splint out of bark and twine."

"We'll swear off men."

"Fifty years from now, there will be legends about the women of the woods. People will say, 'They clothe themselves in woven fern. They walk shoulder to shoulder through the trees, plucking wildflowers from stems. They shed dried pine needles like breadcrumbs.'"

We could still feel the magic of last night tingling through our fingers.

In a couple days, our boyfriends would get worried. They'd drive up the mountain and meet each other at Joan's cabin, at the address we'd given them in the case of an emergency. They'd smell the beastliness on each other and realize the secret we'd been keeping. But still, they'd come looking for us. They'd follow our scent through the trees. They'd find us at our cabin, sitting in the sun, chewing on the last of our granola bars.

Or maybe they wouldn't.

Maybe the rain washed away our scent.

Every summer, wildfires striped the mountain like slug trails. But there would always be dark, hidden spaces the fires couldn't reach. Maybe we would live on in this cabin. If someone were to stumble upon us, they'd find windows curtained in strung-together woodpecker feathers. Strips of meat drying on a shoestring. The cabin would expand and contract, cracks opening and closing, depending on the time of year. Slow breaths that took a whole season to complete.

The desert below would grow dryer and hotter than ever. The mountain would become an island for more than just the bear and foxes, though most wouldn't know it. Only those who watched for years—years of continuous, quiet watching—would catch a glimpse of the secret creatures that hid behind the trees.

The Woman Through the Door

THINGS GO MISSING in the nursing home.

Helen's weighted blanket. A letter from her late husband. An abalone button. A cassette tape of crashing waves she bought at Acadia National Park after she stepped into the ocean for the first time, age fifty-two. A cassette player. A scratchy afghan knitted by she-forgets-who. A photo of herself as a child, mummy-wrapped in jackets and scarves, taken that winter the snow fell so hard it vanished the mailbox, the garden gate, the rhododendron bushes.

When Helen came to live in the nursing home, a few months ago now, the staff warned her. They said sometimes residents would get confused and wander away with other people's belongings. Don't worry, they said. It's never malicious. So, Helen tried to prepare. She labeled her objects with a black Sharpie. HELEN. In large all-caps, so even her roommate, half-blind Lois, could read it. Their doors don't lock, so she hid important objects between her mattress and bedframe, tucked under the edges of the fitted sheet.

Still, one by one, her items disappeared. She'd go for a slow walk around the building, or go to dinner with the other ladies in her hall, and she'd return to a blank feeling in her room and an empty space on the dresser or under the mattress.

It was never more than an annoyance until the day her rock disappeared. It wasn't an especially valuable rock, but she'd had it since childhood. She'd found it in a creek when she was twelve or thirteen. A rock that fit perfectly in her palm and was almost completely smooth, except for one thin crack she'd pick at with her thumbnail. For nearly eight decades she'd managed to not lose it, to take it with her through the transitions in her life. She thought she'd die with it one day, its familiar weight in her pocket.

Helen felt the rock missing the moment she returned to her room from lunch. When she shoved her hand inside the pillowcase where she kept it hidden, her instinct was confirmed.

Helen couldn't understand it. Who stole a rock from another person's pillow?

She decided she would find it. Helen looked in the rec room, under the air hockey table and inside the carboard boxes holding puzzle pieces. She looked in the television room, making sure to check between and under the couch cushions. She went to the dining hall, where the staff was still cleaning up lunch, where tables were decorated with vases of flowers that looked real but smelled like nothing.

There was only one last place in the nursing home to search: the sunroom. No one liked going in the sunroom. Because one, it smelled like Florida and two, it was where the parrot lived. When Helen thought about it, it was the perfect place to hide things you didn't want found.

As Helen stepped into the sunroom, the parrot clamored beak-and-claw across his massive cage to greet her. The parrot's name was Steve. On his cage, there was a sign that said, "Therapy Parrot on the Job," which everyone thought must be a joke. The parrot was more likely to bite than to comfort. He was the type of parrot that was supposed to speak, but as far as Helen knew, never had. A couple weeks ago, someone had passed around an article during dinner about a macaw that had just celebrated his 117th birthday. The article unsettled and depressed them. They didn't like thinking about the fact that Steve would outlive them all, would probably still be rattling his bars and biting knuckles when they were nothing but ash in a box.

Helen shuffled around Steve's cage. "Out with it, Steven," she said, craning her neck to see into the shadows behind the potted plants. "Where'd they put it?"

Steve turned his bead-black eye in her direction and said nothing.

"Don't be so withholding," Helen chided.

She combed through the room, looking under every chair, under the leaves of every potted plant. She even scanned the bottom of the parrot's cage, searching for the glint of something familiar amidst the bird shit and lost feathers. She was about to give up and move on when she noticed a door.

It was a white paneled door on an out-facing wall. This was strange for a couple of reasons. Firstly, she didn't remember ever seeing the door before. Secondly, she knew that this side of the nursing home was bordered by a thick wall of holly, meaning the door would have to open straight into the leaves and branches.

Maybe she was wrong, though. Maybe the door led to a small supply closet. Maybe that was where someone had chosen to hide her stolen things.

Helen stepped forward, put a hand on the knob.

Steve let out a wild parrot scream and banged his beak against one of his bell toys.

"Shush," she said over her shoulder.

She pushed the door open. She stepped through.

⁂

The door, just so you know, and Helen's passage through it, is not a metaphor for death.

The door is real.

For the past few months, starting right before her move to the home, Helen had been noticing that her mind would occasionally time travel. Never for more than a few seconds. And she always knew when it was happening. Sometimes it would bring things from the past into the present. Great Aunt Maribel's cigarette burning on her windowsill. Her husband in his Air Force uniform, leaving for the Sioux Falls

Army Air Field, not looking back as he shut the door behind him. Her old spaniel, Blaze, barking from another room. A chicken coop, strewn feathers moving with the breeze. An inherited perfume bottle, stopper shaped like a ballerina. Tulip bulbs as round and warm as eggs passed from her mother's hands to hers.

I'm telling you; the door was not like that.

The door is not a metaphor and the door is not a figment of Helen's imagination. The door is real for her, and the door would be real for you, too. If you'd been there.

❧

Helen's palms hurt.

She was on her hands and knees on the other side of the door, which appeared to have shut behind her. She didn't remember the door closing. She also didn't remember falling.

Helen stood up slowly and brushed the dirt off her hands. She wasn't in a supply closet like she'd expected. She was in a meadow surrounded by thick, coniferous trees. She could smell the sharp snap of pine. Bees buzzed out of sight, hidden by foxtails as tall as Helen's hips. Though she couldn't locate the sun, the sky was bright and blue.

This place was entirely unfamiliar.

Helen's skin prickled with heat. She picked at her turtleneck and curled her toes inside her slippers. In the nursing home, she was always cold, no matter the season. She rolled up her sleeves and pushed her hair away from her neck.

She thought about what to do next.

Behind her, the door's knob glinted in the bright light. It'd be so easy to go back. She was sure she wasn't supposed to be here.

But she hadn't accomplished her mission yet. And on the other side of the clearing, the trees parted slightly as though for a path. Through the parted trunks, the shade of the forest looking as sweet as the deepest part of a creek. It made Helen's mouth water, and before she was aware of making the decision to move towards it, her feet were carrying her.

The shade of the forest engulfed her. It smelled of chlorophyl and rot and new life. As Helen's eyes adjusted to the darkness, a cabin took shape on the path ahead of her. A small cabin, made of roughly hewn logs, barely bigger than the room Helen shared back at the nursing home. One side of the cabin was missing a wall and opened to the forest. Helen could see dried herbs tied with string hanging from the ceiling. A cast iron pot, as big as a laundry basket, balanced on a frame over blackened wood. Helen stepped closer, wanting to see what was inside.

"Hello?" A woman spoke from a cot on the other side of the room.

"Oh, I'm sorry," Helen said, quickly stepping back. She felt betrayed finding someone else here, in the forest. For a moment she'd believed it was all hers. "Are you staff? I was just looking for something I lost."

The woman had white hair pulled into a bun. Uneven teeth. High cheek bones that made her eyes look sunken. She got out of the cot slowly, like she had to consider the movement of each muscle, each bone.

Finally, she settled herself in front of Helen. She squinted at her, up and down. "Well," she exclaimed, "you're just as old as I am."

Helen didn't mind being called old. For the most part, she'd enjoyed aging. She liked how age softened her expression. She liked when young women in their thirties or forties, just starting to feel the early edge of age, smiled at her in the grocery stores. She liked that being old meant she'd survived a lot. Sometimes she thought about how the only thing she hadn't experienced yet was death, but that it couldn't be any worse than some of the other things she'd experienced.

As the woman continued examining Helen, Helen took the opportunity to look into the cast iron pot.

In its belly, she could see some sprigs of rosemary, a handful of capless acorns. Also, there was an afghan. A button. A cassette tape. A folded piece of paper. A single, round stone.

"Oh," she said. She didn't know whether to be angry or relieved. Had this woman stolen her items or found them? She looked at the woman again, took in her clothes. She wore a long, beige, shapeless dress that stopped just above her thin, yellowing ankles. "You don't work here, do you?" Helen said, now accusatory. "You don't belong at the home."

The woman smiled. "You don't belong there either, Helen." Her front teeth overlapped. She was missing a canine. When a wasp buzzed into the cabin and landed in her hair, she didn't swat it away.

Helen wondered what was happening. Was this woman a thief? A squatter? She'd read about intruders who lived in people's walls, their basements, for years, remaining undiscovered by only coming out at night. Taking one egg. One slice of bread. Things that would go unnoticed.

"Who are you? What is this place?" Helen asked. "I've never noticed it here before."

The woman smiled wider. "Helen, don't lie. You know this place."

Helen was about to protest, but as soon as the woman said it, she realized it was true. Or partially true. She didn't know this place. But she knew parts of this place. These pine trees with their wide bases were the same she'd hidden beneath when she was a child playing hide and seek with the neighborhood kids. She'd kissed a boy for the first time under such a tree. Afterwards, the skin on their arms was strange and unfamiliar, bumpy with the pattern of fallen pine needles. She'd run home, afraid her friends would see their matching patterns and know what they'd done.

And this cabin. It wasn't really a cabin. It was the shed in the backyard of her first adult home in Muncy, Pennsylvania where she'd stored gardening equipment. She wondered what had become of her tomato garden. She wondered if tulips still bloomed. She wondered if anyone still put out a salt lick for the white-tailed deer. She'd rented the home by herself, which was unusual for a woman in those days. She'd relished waking up every morning to no one, to empty rooms that were only for her to fill.

Even this woman's voice seemed suddenly familiar. The woman had an inflection that reminded Helen of friends she'd made in typing school. Friends who'd, like her, grown up in factory towns. Women whose brothers worked in the glass factories, sometimes came home with missing fingers. Women who'd endured cold winters, walked to school with ankles wet from slush and shoes white with road salt.

Helen shook her head. Rubbed her eyes. She started to reach for her things at the bottom of the pot, but the woman stopped her.

"These are the things you must sacrifice, if you are to stay and I am to leave."

"Stay," Helen repeated, not understanding.

The woman sighed. A wind blew, and there was the soft patter of pine needles hitting the room. When the woman spoke, her tone was softer than it was before, like a mother explaining something difficult to a child. "Helen, one day someone else will come to these woods, and it will be their turn to stay and your time to go. But that won't be for a long time, not until you're ready."

Helen looked over her shoulder. On the other side of the clearing, she could still see the white door that led back to the nursing home. Though it was becoming fuzzy. Like something her eyes couldn't focus on. She didn't want to go back. She didn't want the final home of her life to be a building full of strangers, didn't want to pretend to be comforted by a parrot that wouldn't even speak. If she had to die eventually, she'd rather do it here. Amongst the woodpeckers and the fungi growing up the trunks of the trees and the plants converting sunlight to sugar. She'd rather this be her final home.

The woman smiled and nodded. "Well then," she said.

She turned, and then she was gone.

Helen blinked. She searched the room, walked outside and circled the cabin. Went back inside.

Her things—the blanket, the cassette, the letter, the stone—had gone, too.

She sat on the edge of the bed. When she lay down into it, the hollow in the center of the mattress perfectly fit the shape of her body. A breeze passed through the cabin, swinging the hanging herbs. She heard the spiders stepping along the edges of the shutters. A mouse scratched across the roof.

Helen got up out of bed.

There was much to do. She had a bunch of tomatoes, freshly picked from the garden, that needed washing. She had a chicken coop to repair before the martins came to steal the eggs. She had tulip bulbs to dig up before the frost came. So much to do. There would be time for sleep later.

Hex

ALL WINTER, my ex-wife has been flying around the countryside, cursing people and farms. She rides a broom made from a pine branch, twigs hot-glued to the end. She only appears after midnight. She cackles down people's chimney, and by the time they put on their glasses and slippers and robes and stumble out onto their iced-over porches, she's gone.

It's awkward for me. Our friends, who all chose me after the split, call up to complain of odd, annoying curses. A left nostril that always needs to sneeze but never does. A prized hen that has started laying hollow eggs that give off a bad stench when cracked. Hair that is constantly staticky, even, somehow, when wet.

We get together for sushi in the next town over, and my friends laugh about how my ex-wife has taken to wearing a black cloak and pointed hat. "So cliché! I saw her in a check-out line at Whole Foods with a basket full of chanterelle mushrooms. I think she's started to tint her skin green. I heard she does it by bathing with foxglove." "I hear she's living on that island in the swamp." "I think she's dating a goblin."

I laugh along with them. I shake my head like I can't believe it and lay a strip of nigiri on my tongue. I don't tell my friends that eating sushi kind of makes me miss my witchy wife. She was the one who taught me how to eat raw fish. She knew my favorite part of the meal was the *crack* of splitting the single-use chopsticks, and would always let me split hers for her.

My single friends tell me I should start dating again. They offer to set me up with their cousins, with their neighbors, with their doctor, with their favorite bartender. They know a girl with purple hair whose hobby is sword fighting. They know a girl who makes her own furniture. They know a girl who owns a parrot with green feathers that sings pop songs on command. "The world is full of girls," they say, "who won't hex you when you break up with them."

When we were married, my ex-wife's magic was attractive and helpful. She'd bathe crystals in citrine bowls so our tomatoes would grow round and fat. She'd burn runes onto the crests of mink skulls and place them on the windowsill to protect our home from mold. She'd bathe in oils and herbs and come to bed with bits of damp lavender stuck to the back of her neck and creosote pressed behind her knees. Her hair was black and long and would catch on twigs and bushes when we went on walks through the woods. Sometimes at night, she'd levitate under the blankets. I'd awake to a draft and reach up to her, pull her back down to me.

It wasn't all good, though. She tended to say the wrong things. She insulted people without realizing she was doing it. She looked bored at family holiday parties, refused to hold babies, would cut conversations short by giving only "yes" or "no" answers to questions. She couldn't give a convincing apology. She melted black wax onto every table top and windowsill in our home and forgot to clean it up. She clogged our shower drain with rosemary. We'd have arguments that would last through the night and end with us lying side by side in bed, cold morning light parting the space between us.

I found myself constantly making excuses for her to my friends, before they even asked for excuses. "She's just weird in crowds," I'd say. "She's an introvert," I'd say. Once I saw a therapist who told me I was too worried about how my relationship appeared on the outside, and it wasn't fair that I was projecting my insecurities onto my partner. I stopped going after that. I always felt like I was lying in therapy. Nothing I said about myself ever felt true enough.

After sushi, a friend gives me a lift home. I wave as he backs out of my drive, then sit down heavily on my front stoop. It's almost midnight, and I'm drunk on sake and beer. I feel the alcohol buzzing in my cheeks, in my palms, in my fingertips. I feel like if I snap my fingers, they might zap with electricity.

My house, which used to be our house, sits on the edge of a hill. From here I can look down on the forest below. My ex-wife and I used to have competitions to see who could spot the first bat flitting above the trees at dusk. "It's bat o'clock!" we'd say, when we found the first one. The bats migrated south months ago. But I wonder if, tonight, I'll see my ex-wife skimming above the trees.

The truth is, I haven't seen her since the day I suggested we divorce. We were sitting right here. She was looking out over the forest, her hair concealing her face from me. After I told her, she got up without a word, went into the house. I gave her a few minutes, then followed. But she was already gone. Vanished. Her herbs and oils and crystals and vials along with her. A glimmer of black smoke in the air.

My friends assume she's hexed me. Not because of anything I've said, but because it's the sort of thing they expect her to do.

But she hasn't hexed me.

She curses my friends, strangers, but never me.

My friend said she'd heard a rumor that my ex-wife is living in the swamp north of town. I know the place, beyond the train tracks, where the trees grow taller and quieter. We used to go on fall drives and stop by the side of the road and walk until the earth turned to mud and every step felt like a dare. Eventually one of us would fall through the mud to our shins, and then the game would be over and we could turn back.

My ex-wife loved the swamp with its hidden traps and sweet-smelling reeds. She'd always find treasures in the mud to carry back home with us. A snake's skin. A crow's feather.

I wonder if the rumor is true.

I wonder if I could find her there.

Maybe if I were to find her and talk to her, she'd stop cursing my friends. I'm the reason she started plaguing them in the first place. I've got to try. It's the right thing to do.

I'm too drunk to get in the car, but behind my house is my old bike. I kick the wheels where they've frozen to the ground, and then I am off. The winter air tears at my cheeks. I focus on my pedaling, so I don't overthink what I'm doing and change my mind. As I bike, the clouds part. The moon is an empty bowl. Somewhere a rooster crows in a barn.

I reach the swamp and drop my bike by the side of the road. I stagger through the tall, quiet trees until the ground turns to mud.

In the swamp, there is no snow. Steam rises from the ground and then refreezes in the tree branches, coating the twigs like sticks of rock candy. I walk until the mud no longer supports my weight, until I start to feel myself sinking up to my ankles, to my shins. That is when I see it. A hut on an island in the mud. I'd never noticed it before, but it looks like it's always been there, moss draped over the roof, the front stoop blanketed with damp leaves.

I try to walk towards it, but my feet are stuck in the mud. They make an ugly suction-cup sound as I try to unstick myself from the ground.

I notice an orange, flickering glow from one of the hut's windows.

"Hello!" I speak. My voice sounds flat and tinny in the quiet swamp. "Hello," I say again. "Come out."

At the beginning of our relationship, I loved that my ex-wife never went out of her way to make people like her. I never had to worry that she was being dishonest about her feelings for me. I never had that squirmy feeling in my stomach, like I had with other women, that she was performing, that there was a truer version of herself she kept hidden. It was only later that this became a quality I resented. "Why can't you just pretend to be having a good time?" I'd whisper. "Just try."

Nothing moves inside the cabin. Why doesn't she come to the window? Why doesn't she stomp out the front door, enchant a swarm of hornets to chase me away?

"I see you," I lie. "I need to talk to you."

I try again to take a step closer to the hut, but my feet stick in the mud and I fall. I land on my hands and knees and stay there for a moment, elbow-deep in mud, catching my breath, feeling the cold numb my skin. I see how pathetic I must look like from the outside.

How cliché. A drunk who took his partner for granted. But I don't think I'm drunk. Not anymore.

I struggle to my feet. "Shit," I say. "It wasn't supposed to be like this. You were supposed to fight me. You were supposed to curse me. You were supposed to send a plague of snakes to my bedside, or make it rain rocks whenever I tried to leave the house, or haunt my dreams. You weren't supposed to just leave."

For a moment I think it will work. She'll appear in the doorway in all her rage and power. Tall and long-limbed, black hair hanging in knots, energy crackling between her fingers, a necklace of bones cackling around her neck. She'll be everything she was with me and more. My ex-wife, the witch.

A breeze moves over the swamp. The trees bend, like they're exhaling. I exhale with them. The mud dries and cracks on my forearms. Everything is very quiet.

The Last Glacier

LATER, I WILL IMAGINE IT LIKE THIS: Under the soft, pink glow of midnight sun, my husband leaves our tent. In his boots, wool hat, and pajamas, but nothing else, he follows the edge of the lagoon. The glacier accordion-folds along the opposite side of the water, jagged and shaded in black, volcanic sand. He feels himself stumbling towards it. Drawn to its size, like a passing asteroid suddenly caught in the earth's gravitational pull.

When he reaches the glacier, he climbs until he can stand. The sun buffers along the horizon beyond the ice. It's June in Iceland, and this is as dark as it will get until August. The ice glitters, unfolding before him with each step, a great plain of white. He doesn't turn around. He keeps walking.

☙

When I wake in the morning and find my husband's sleeping bag cold, I'm disoriented. I take a moment to place myself on the globe: Southeastern Iceland. Six hours, by car, outside of Reykjavik. A campground at the base of the country's last remaining glacier.

My watch tells me it's 7 AM.

"Honey?" I call through the tent, to no reply.

I wonder if he's started up the camp stove and is boiling water for coffee. Or maybe he's taken a walk to the outhouse. His coat and messenger bag, containing the rental car keys, our passports, and maps, are still in the tent next to me, so he couldn't have gone far.

I unzip the flap, leaving the bubble of warmth, and step into the brisk, foggy morning. About ten tents line the bank of the lagoon, like brightly colored boulders contrasting the black sand. The outhouse near the parking lot is open, the door swinging in the breeze. Other campers are already up and starting their mornings, more shape than human—bundled in wool sweaters, in parkas, in scarves.

My husband is not among them.

⁂

Friends suggested we go to Hawaii for our honeymoon. Or to a resort in Mexico. I said those were boring ideas. I wanted beaches with waves that could drag me out to sea. I wanted rugged shorelines, North Atlantic winds that could scrub me hollow. I wanted hands shoved into each other's pockets for warmth, rain pounding on the windshield. I wanted our world to be shrunk to me and him and the shape of the car, to the concave of a tent, to the parabola of a single umbrella.

My husband had laughed. He said it sounded romantic.

So, we bought plane tickets. Reserved a car with four-wheel-drive. Rented camping gear.

The plan was to take ten days to circle the entire island, counterclockwise. We'd soak in geothermal rivers, climb the spines of sleeping volcanoes, eat fermented shark in fishing villages. I taught myself common Icelandic phrases. I made lists of the highest rated restaurants in each village we'd visit. We had a strict schedule to keep to, in order to get through all we'd planned.

But then, we saw Vatnajökull.

Only five hours into our trip: a white line running between green mountain tops and blue sky. We couldn't keep our eyes off it. As we got closer, the line of white thickened. Streams of glacier melt streaked the hillsides like veins of gemstones in a mine.

We followed signs to a campground that ended up just being a lagoon beach with a single outhouse infested with black midges. But it bordered the ice. We could walk up and put our palms to it. We could dip our faces into the melt and let it fill our ears. We hadn't reached our destination for the day. When we'd drawn up plans, we'd given ourselves just enough time to take a picture of Vatnajökull from an overlook next to the highway. But now that we were seeing it—glittering, massive, cold—we couldn't seem to get ourselves to leave. We decided we'd stay and make up for lost time tomorrow.

⁊⅋

Around lunchtime, a woman packing up her tent at the next campsite over notices me sitting in my camping chair alone. She shouts over in Icelandic.

"Sorry," I say, and she switches effortlessly into English: "Where is your man?"

When I tell her I haven't seen him since last night, she is more concerned than I've allowed myself to become. It's been five hours since I woke and found him missing.

"He probably went on a walk and," I begin, and she cuts me off.

"No, no, no. This isn't a good place to be gone on your own. You could slip on smooth ice and crack your head. You could be crushed in a collapsing ice cave. You could fall into a crevasse, be swallowed by quicksand."

I've been pacing the beach all morning, telling myself that, unable to sleep under the nighttime sun, he'd gone on a hike. Or tried to walk to the closest village for supplies—he left his wallet, but maybe he brought cash—and lost track of time. But explaining this out loud, I realize how flippant, or how naïve, it makes me sound.

"Don't worry," the woman says. "I'll call."

She sits with me as we wait for the national park emergency services to arrive.

"I'm Margret." She shakes my hand. Her skin is cold and smooth. She is young and blonde and willowy.

Margret tells me she's employed by the tourism board. She travels the country and makes videos about Icelandic destinations from a local's perspective.

"Want to see?"

Before I answer, she turns her phone to me. In all her videos, she wears a wool sweater and a red beanie. She is bare-faced and young. She gives peace signs next to baying sheep on dirt roads. She models a long, black, twill skirt she calls a peysuföt, traditional Icelandic garb. She leaps joyously under a rainbow at the base of a waterfall. Each video clip is no more than a few seconds. I recognize some of the places my husband and I meant to travel.

I feel my stomach churn.

❧

Neither of us had seen a glacier in real life before. Hardly anyone has. A decade ago, when it was clear they would soon be gone, glacier tourism briefly boomed in the United States for the upper and upper middle class. Everyone wanted a piece of the last glaciers. They brought coolers to Glacier National Park, to Glacier Bay, and chipped off blocks of ice to take home. Clickbait articles named celebrities who had ice sculptures made from the now-extinct Perito Moreno, cocktail ice cubes from the Baltoro in Pakistan.

So, the national parks closed, or at least closed to visitors. They protected the pieces of glaciers that remained.

We were not among the people, at the time, who could afford to visit the ice. Glaciers had always seemed like distant, mythical things to us. We'd both grown up knowing that—like bumblebees, like the Great Barrier Reef, like the streets of Venice—they were not long for this world. So instead of grieving them, we tried to consider them already gone.

§

That night, I turn my phone off airplane mode.

The search team wanted me to be accessible in case of updates. They also told me it's best if I stay here at the campground, in case he returns.

When he returns, I edited in my mind.

There were four of them in yellow vests, all business. They asked questions that felt accusatory. *No, we weren't drinking,* I told them. *No, there was no drug use. No, we hadn't been fighting. No, he didn't share any plans with me.*

They didn't comfort me or tell me it would be okay. I wondered how many tourists they'd had to rescue from the glacier over the course of their careers. How many had they found alive? I wanted to tell them my husband and I were different. We respected the land, understood its power. But I didn't have any evidence of that.

For dinner, I forced down some sausage and a roll that concerned fellow campers shared with me—once the emergency services left, everyone wanted to talk to me, to reassure me. Then, I crawled inside the tent and into my husband's sleeping bag.

As soon as airplane mode goes off, my phone lights up with "have fun on your trip" messages from friends and family members back in the States. I text them pictures I took with my husband yesterday, and say we're having a great time.

Then, I research glaciers.

I learn that glaciers used to cover about 10% of Iceland but now barely 1%.

I learn that Vatnajökull is an average of 250 meters deep, though just a decade ago it was almost 100 meters more.

I learn that under all that ice is a volcano that creates flooding glacial lakes when it erupts.

I learn that when a glacier releases an iceberg, it's called calving.

I learn that to earn the term glacier, jökull in Icelandic, the ice needs to be thick enough to travel, slowly, under the force of its own weight. A glacier is only a glacier as long as it's moving.

My husband and I met at a mutual friend's pool party. We lived in Tucson, and it was summer, so a pool was necessary for socializing.

We floated in the deep end, each draped over one side of a pool noodle. I felt the skin on my ears burning, but I didn't want to pause our conversation to reapply sunscreen.

I learned that he, like I, had grown up here. We'd both watched as the population steadily shrank, whole neighborhoods going vacant as families moved north, to cities that hadn't yet had to put limits on water usage, to states with shorter and cooler summers. Even our parents had left. Mine lived in an apartment in Michigan, his in Minnesota.

Tucson had survived the changes better than other Arizona cities, by adopting traditional Tohono O'odham agricultural practices, by banning turf lawns and equipping homes with water harvesting barrels.

But still, you could feel the end coming. Deep, wide fissures split across the desert like stretch marks, formed when groundwater was pumped from the aquifers much more quickly than nature could replenish them. The mountains to the north of the city burned at night, and when we woke there would be new streaks of red from where flame-retardant chemicals had been dropped from drones.

"Why are you still here?" I asked him.

"Someone needs to be here to witness the end," he said, and smiled like it was a joke.

I wake in the middle of the night, and for a moment, I hope it's because my husband has returned. But when I pull back my eye mask, I'm still alone.

I didn't zipper the door flap completely before falling asleep, and a thread of wind whispers inside. The tent expands and contracts around me like a giant lung.

I reach for the zipper, and instead of closing the door, I unzip the flap and step outside in my bare feet.

No one else is up. Yesterday's fog has cleared, and wisps of pink lick across the sky.

I see a helicopter flying low over the glacier in the distance. I wonder if it's the search team, looking for my husband. He's been missing for an entire day now.

I slip on my boots, pull on a sweater, and walk to the edge of the water. The color of the water is milky. Chunks of ice float across it like paper cranes. I follow the footprints in the black sand to the edge of the glacier, where there are signs warning hikers to go no farther without a guide, to stop unless prepared with the proper equipment.

I step beyond the sign but walk just to the point where sand becomes snow. When I place my palm on the glacier, the ice immediately starts to melt under the warmth of my skin. I tap my fingers against it, imagining I can send a vibration that will web its way to my husband.

⁊⁊

It's been three days, and there's still been no sign of him.

In four more days, we are scheduled to fly home.

The head of the search team calls me to ask for updates. I have none, and neither does he.

I spend my day pacing the campsite and the beach, watching the sun skim across the sky, or sitting in the rental car listening to oldies on the radio. The songs are in English, but the DJ speaks in Icelandic.

In the early afternoon, a group of a dozen hikers gathers at the base of the glacier. I sidle up, listening as the guide explains how dangerous the ice can be. "During the summer thaw, it's hard to predict where sink holes have formed, or where the ice has thinned. Stakes tied with red ribbons mark the safe path. Don't stray."

She passes out hard hats and crampons to strap onto their boots, and I don't stop her when she hands them out to me.

I take up the back of the line, worried that any moment she'll realize I am not part of the group. As she leads us onto the glacier, a piece of ice the size of a car breaks off and bobs into the lagoon.

"See," she says. "The glacier is an unpredictable animal."

The guide is a middle-aged woman with a German accent. She has sun-freckled skin and a loud voice.

As we get used to the feel of the crampons clinging to the ice, she tells us about the first dead glacier, declared in 2014. "It was called Okjökull. Glaciologists can estimate the age of a glacier by counting its rings, layers of dust accumulated each year. They determined that Okjökull was only a few centuries old when it died. Just a baby, by glacier standards. And now, it is just a pile of slush."

She told us Iceland held a memorial service at the base of the quiet volcano that was once Okjökull, now only Ok. A death certificate was read. A plaque was placed.

I want to ask if the glaciers that died after Okjökull also had funerals, but I don't want to draw attention to myself.

A world of ice unfolds ahead of me. Peaks, valleys, plains of rippled white, all outlined in volcanic dust. I wonder if my husband thought to follow the marked trail when he wandered off that night. Or if he followed the midnight sun. Or if, hypnotized by the glacier, he didn't follow any discernable path at all.

I'm falling behind the rest of the group, and I let the gap between us widen. No one turns around looking for me, their eyes fixed either on the path or the horizon ahead of them.

I sit down on the ice, letting the cold seep through my jeans.

The glacier hums beneath my feet.

I moved in with my husband after six months of dating. He lived in his childhood home, which his parents had been unable to sell when they left the state. Evidence of his past was everywhere. Sharpie marks on a doorframe marking his growth. Pinholes in the walls of his childhood room, from where he hung movie and band posters. A chip in the kitchen tile from when he dropped his rock collection. Layers upon layers of paint on the walls that went back to before his family even lived here, each coat marking a different occupant.

We painted over them in yet another shade, adding our own layer to the house's history.

We bought new furniture. We hung new curtains.

Behind the house was a wash, a path for the monsoon rains to take in late summer. My husband said that when he was a kid, the wash would sometimes flow like a stream for weeks. But it'd been over a decade since it had last tasted water.

Some nights we walked down the wash like it was a trail. The other houses on the block are empty, and the wash took us by their backyards. We snooped on empty swimming pools, courtyards overgrown with cholla, husks of sailboats buzzing with wasps.

Other nights, my husband said he wanted to be alone. He'd disappear into the moonlit dark for an hour or more and come back with fingertips sticky with creosote and devil's claws clinging to his shoelaces.

The desert clung to him, and he clung back.

The other hikers are gone, disappeared around a hill of ice in the distance.

I imagine at some point they'll stop, and the guide will do a headcount. I was never meant to be part of the group, so they won't notice me missing at first. They probably won't notice me missing until they've returned to the lagoon and the guide realizes she's lost a hat and pair of crampons.

I step off the trail, carefully, and climb uphill for a better view.

To the east, a patch of bright blue ice glints against the white. I learned in my glacier research that only the deepest or densest glacier ice is blue, so people usually only see it where the ice has cracked, revealing its deeper parts. I picture my husband stuck in a chasm, the ice numbing his skin, and head in that direction.

I stop often, worn out by the effort of stomping the crampons into the ice and then shaking them loose again for each step. The upside is that I'm leaving myself a trail to follow back.

It takes me almost an hour to reach the blue I'd spotted in the distance. An hour off the marked, safe trail.

I find myself at the mouth of an ice cave. The entrance is barely wider than my shoulders, but I can tell that it is bigger inside.

"Hello," I call in.

Feet first, I slide carefully through the opening. The cave is the size of a walk-in closet. The ice is smooth and rippled and a deep, turquoise blue. Ahead of me, another opening leads to a tunnel. Just inside, I see a limp, wool hat.

I rush over to grab it. It's gray, made of thick, crocheted, strands of wool yarn. I recognize it immediately.

My husband was here.

I put the hat on my head and get on my hands and knees to crawl through the tunnel. It's like crawling through a hall of stained glass. Light pulses through the ice, and the blue deepens, reminds me of videos of skies just before a tornado.

I take a moment to rest, and in the stillness, I'm sure I can hear a sound coming from deeper in the ice. I put my ear to it and think I can hear a heartbeat. A gurgling. Like when you rest your ear on your partner's stomach and are suddenly reminded that they are made of flesh and blood and moving inner parts.

I crawl faster.

❧

I never followed my husband when he went out into the desert alone. I always trusted that he would come back. But maybe he wanted me to join him, to be willing to walk out into the dark and find him amongst the fanged and spined dangers.

As the tunnel begins to slope downward, I remember the guide's words about how scientists can measure the age of glaciers by looking for the layers of dust.

How many decades deep am I?

Have I passed the year when humanity reached the point of no return in global warming?

The year the first Viking ship struck sand on the coast of Iceland?
The year the last mammoth had its last meal?

I crawl backwards along the timeline, trying to catch up with my husband. When I find him, we won't leave the glacier. We'll keep crawling deeper. We'll subsist on the minerals in the ice. We'll stay with the glacier until the melting reaches us.

Acknowledgments

Thank you to the journals where iterations of these stories first appeared: *Pithead Chapel, Mid-American Review, Not Deer Magazine, Juked, Jellyfish Review, Splice, Cartridge Lit, Waxwing, Ghost Parachute, MudRoom, Doubleback Review,* and *Invisible City.*

Thank you to Sam Martone, who recommended I visit Walter De Maria's exhibit, *The New York Earth Room,* which inspired the title story in this collection.

Thank you to the friends who read my first drafts and helped me see their potential: Melissa Goodrich, Elizabeth Deanna Morris Lakes, Ingrid Wenzler, Reneé Bibby, Jackie Balderrama, and Sam Martone.

Thank you to David Byron Queen and my friends in the word west workshops for their thoughtful feedback and enthusiasm for Wes Anderson and David Lynch films and ghosts.

Thank you to the Sundress Academy for the Arts for giving me a porch and a hayloft to write in for a week. Thank you to Signal Fire, for leading me into the Klamath-Siskiyou wilderness.

Thank you to my desert coven and to my forever-housemates.

Thank you to my family, for taking me into the woods and teaching me to look closely at the world. Thank you to my mom, for reading me stories and making the world feel magical.

Thank you, always, to Will. With you, life is brighter.

DANA DIEHL is the author of *Our Dreams Might Align* (Splice UK, 2018) and the collaborative collection, *The Classroom* (Gold Wake Press, 2019). Her chapbook, *TV Girls*, won the 2017-2018 New Delta Review Chapbook Contest judged by Chen Chen. Diehl earned her MFA in Fiction at Arizona State University. Her work has appeared in *North American Review, Necessary Fiction, Mid-American Review*, and elsewhere. She is an educator in Tucson.